FUTUREWORDS:
A BRICK CAVE ANTHOLOGY

EDITED BY:
HARMONY NELSON

Brick Cave Books
brickcavebooks.com
2017

Cover Composite Photo by tolokonov.
Cover Composite Design by Bob Nelson.

Brick Cave Media
brickcavemedia.com
2015

Published by Brick Cave Books
Mesa, AZ
2017

FUTUREWORDS:
A BRICK CAVE ANTHOLOGY

EDITED BY:
HARMONY NELSON

Brick Cave Books
brickcavebooks.com
2017

FOREWARD

From Editor Harmony Nelson

I remember the first time I read a sci-fi fantasy novel. I was in third grade, and it was Madeleine L'Engle's *A Wrinkle in Time*. I was quickly and thoroughly hooked on both sci-fi and fantasy genres and spent several years thereafter completely immersed. My collection of fantasy ranged from J.K. Rowling's *Harry Potter* to Robert Jordan's *The Wheel of Time*. I read the classics, like T.H. White's *The Once and Future King* and J.R.R. Tolkien's *Lord of the Rings*. My favorite books in class at school were always sci-fi. I loved Ray Bradbury's *Fahrenheit 451* and George Orwell's *Nineteen Eighty-four*. I loved Harry Harrison's *Stainless Steel Rat* series (but I'll admit I was too young to understand a lot of the jokes). What I mean to say by sharing this with you is that my most relevant experience as the editor of this anthology is my experience with a love for reading, and a love for the sci-fi and fantasy genres.

Futurewords: A Brick Cave Anthology has the same variety of voices and stories that I loved when

I was a kid. Everything is here, from the transformative young love in Collette Black's "Swan's Petition" to the laugh-out-loud satire in Scott Wood's "Second Coming Soon."

Sharon Skinner delivers a powerful heroine's struggle with identity that leaves you wondering in "Sacrilege." Reading this story reminded me of watching an M. Night Shyamalan movie (one of the good ones). I felt immediately connected to the tale of a young woman searching for her true identity. Skinner effortlessly blends her story with elements of sci-fi that intrigued my imagination and curiosity. This is one journey you have to read to the end, and even that will leave you wanting more.

J.A. Giunta wrote a story for this anthology reminiscent of some of my favorite short story authors. "Relative" reminds me of the deeply cutting stories George Saunders wrote in his collection, *Tenth of December*. Giunta tackles a great depth of emotion with seemingly effortless simplicity.

Scott Woods' "Second Coming Soon" is not a story to miss. His poignant political satire is as hilarious as it is surprising. Many lines had me laughing out loud, and the whole time I was wondering why this hadn't been done before. Woods takes a great idea and executes it with quick-witted precision in his original story.

Collette Black created a romantic fantasy tale that appeals to my long-standing love for dragons and mythical creatures. What she wrote reminds me of the lovely images and relationships created by some of my favorite Y.A. authors, Suzanne Collins and Naomi Novik.

Bob Nelson's story "Outpost" was like revisiting my favorite episodes of *Star Trek*. His combination of humor and action create a fun story that isn't hard to imagine on the big screen. The story brings together light-hearted adventure with hard-hitting moral questions about relationships with those who are different from us.

I hope when you read this anthology you'll discover what I did. I was ready for an adventure, and I got much more. These stories are fun, clever, sometimes sad, and altogether a lovely collection. I think if you picked up this anthology, you are probably like me. Maybe you grew up loving books, all the books, especially sci-fi and fantasy. Maybe you know what I mean when I say there is a profound joy in exploring written worlds that are impossibly different from yours, but share feelings and experiences you have known in your own life. If that's the case, I know you'll enjoy these stories.

Sharon Skinner

Sharon Skinner holds a B.A. In English, an M.A. in Creative Writing and a Poetic License. She has worked as a landscaper, a cashier, a maid, a waitress, a communications specialist, a videographer, a technical writer, a project management consultant and a biomedical field service engineer and served aboard the USS Jason as one of the first women assigned to a US Navy ship.

Her poetry and fiction have been published in myriad local, national and international publications. Sharon is an active member of SCBWI (Society of Children's Book Writers and Illustrators) and serves as the Regional Advisor for SCBWI AZ.

Her recent publishing credits include In Case You Didn't hear Me the First Time (2010), The Healer's Legacy (2012), The Nelig Stones (2013), Mirabella and the Faded Phantom (March 2014). The highly anticipated sequel to The Healer's Legacy, The Matriarch's Devise, was released in Fall 2015.

On the Web: sharonskinner.com

SACRILEGE
by
Sharon Skinner

Seris stared out at the horizon. Violet sky melted slowly into dusty gray. The bleak landscape reminded her how far from home she was. Never before had she felt so isolated and defeated. Her yellow epan lay dead at her feet. Her dwindling supplies felt inadequate as she lifted her feather-light pack to her shoulder and started off. She would have to go the rest of the way on foot.

The rest of the way.

How far, she wondered, to this sacred place? How long before she would reach the mythical prayer stone?

More importantly, where on this vast arid plain would she find the one thing that could have saved her epan? The one thing that might save her?

Water.

She rechecked her map. Based on the directional reading on her navigator's dial, and if the map was correct—the desert sands were prone to shifting and her equipment practically ancient—she was still heading in the right direction. But after yesterday's sandstorm, she could be miles off course.

Stupid! She'd been so stupid to keep traveling, seeking shelter where there clearly was none.

But she had hoped to save them both. And without water and shelter . . . well, the outcome lay before her.

She would have preferred to bury the sorry little epan. It had been a good companion as well as a sturdy riding beast. But she had no tools for digging, and foragers would only dig him up again. Sadly, she would have to leave him in the open. She needed to keep moving.

The largest of Sala's two white giant suns blazed down from directly overhead now and she repositioned her eye shields to better protect against the glare. If only she had started off closer to an Eighth day, the solar clipsing might have brought some relief from the extreme heat. But how could one plan for a walk into the unknown?

She wondered if the villagers back in Limscon had been right, after all. They had warned her that this journey would prove deadly. But she had not listened. Her need to know had been greater than her fear of death; it still was.

It was, like leaving the epan out in the open, not optional. Not since the dreams had begun.

The dreams, dark visions, almost nightmares, curiously disturbing rather than frightening. They had started after her first kill. She'd had trouble sleeping for several days and when she'd finally fallen into a troubled slumber, the first dark dreams had come to her. They started with a murky void that filled with red lights and shooting stars, turning to a blue haze that filled the sky. Flowers appeared that she had never seen before, shedding a fragrance that consumed her. A fragrance so powerful she could still smell it for hours after she woke.

4

There must be some reason for these strange, uncontrollable dreams. That answer must be found. But the soothsayers had all turned away from her; no one wanted to read her spirit signs for her. No one wanted to touch an unblessed. No one but the strange old hag who lived at the edge of the dunes outside of town.

Everyone Seris met told her Mother Vasquin was crazy, but Seris had gone to the old seer anyway, seeking answers to the questions that had haunted her since she'd been a child.

The ancient hag was blind and dirty, but it was said she could see things that others could not. Whisperers said the gift of sight lay heavy on her. Seris could almost feel the weight of it pushing down on her as she approached the old woman's hut. She stood outside the door for only a moment before reaching up to rap on the splintering planks. But before her knuckles touched wood, she heard a croaking voice call out to her. "Enter seeker, if you dare. Knowledge is power, but also danger."

Seris pushed open the rotting door. It hung from rusted hinges and scraped across the floor, raising dirt and dust to float in the thin rays of sunlight that pierced the cool darkness inside. She hesitated in the doorway, letting her eyes adjust to the gloom, and her nose adjust to the sour smells of age and sweat and rotting food. The old hag sat on the stump of a tree, facing a small wooden table cracked and worn with age. Her back was to the door and Seris could see the bony protrusion of her shoulders through her threadbare robe.

"Come in seeker," the scrawny woman croaked out the words with a dry rasp and began coughing. A rattling cough that shook her entire body. Seris started toward her, but the old crone held up her hand to stop. The cough turned into a choking, retching sound and died off into a wheeze. Finally, the aged woman waved a bony arm at Seris, motioning her to sit on the far side of the table.

Seris stepped into the room, the door swung back, sagged, and stopped. It hung partially open. "Don't worry about the door," wheezed the hag, as Seris walked to the other side of the table. "Not like it keeps anything out. Or anything in for that matter." She chuckled at her own joke, and the coughing started again.

Seris found a stump lying on its side in the dirt near the table and set it on one end. Cautiously, she sat down on it across from the seer, keeping one hand on her belt knife.

"Afraid of a sick old woman, are we?" asked the hag. "Not to worry, mercenary, not much profit in killing the dead." Her words made no sense. Seris wondered if the old witch was simply mad, after all. She watched the woman hunch her shoulders as she sucked in a moaning breath and wondered if she was wasting her time. The seer's face was unreadable. The light that came in through the door behind her outlined her silhouette with an odd nimbus, and her sightless eyes glittered in the dark.

The dark silhouette straightened and sat up. "You seek answers, but none will listen to the questions, eh mercenary? None but the mad. And you wonder if you will be able to sift madness from truth," Mother Vasquin said in a hushed whisper. "You will have to sort that for yourself," she went on. "But first, my fee." She knocked once on the table with her bony knuckles.

Seris reached inside her cloak for her credit clip, but the old woman let out a loud hiss, like a feral tigrin. "No," she said. "Not that. It must be personal, something of worth only to you."

Seris hesitated, remembering. The ring wasn't much, a cheap bauble with no real value. But it was all she had left of her days as a child. A trinket her father had given her on her birthdate. No, not her birthdate, she reminded herself, the date they'd chosen for her, their little stray. She gritted her teeth, pulled the ring roughly from her finger and slapped it down onto the table. The wizened hag snatched it up, clutching it tightly in her bony fist, wheezing loudly as she rocked back and forth. She began babbling, making guttural sounds, then her voice changed, growing louder, deeper. The babbling became words, the words finally forming sentences.

"There is a place for answers," the old woman said in a voice no longer her own. A voice that sent shivers down Seris's spine. "A place where the truth can be found if one is willing to face it. If one is willing to pay the price."

Seris had wondered for a moment if the seer was simply playing into the rumors. The stories had existed for longer than anyone could recall. But Seris had wanted answers. What price could there be beyond what she had already paid? Urged on by Mother Vasquin's words, Seris had been willing and quick to set off on a journey whose end she could not foresee.

Now, here she was in The Desolation, on foot, with little food and no water, her throat already parched. She glanced back, but the epan's carcass was no longer visible against the sandy hillocks. She adjusted her pack and continued on. It would be night in a few hours and she needed to find a place to camp before full dark. Once both suns set, the temperature would drop rapidly.

She marched on, scanning the horizon for signs of shelter, and enemies, needing the first and fearing the second. As a mercenary, it would not be the first time she must fend for herself and possibly defend herself, but she looked on killing with an eye for avoiding it. Spying and fighting might be necessary in her line of work, but killing had left a sour taste in her mouth. A taste she did not wish to experience again soon. If ever.

She reached down, testing the weight of her weapon against her thigh. A simple metal cylinder with a grip on one end and a thumb trigger. It was not as big as most strike blasters, but it was still deadly enough, especially when used with precision. And Seris was always precise.

She thought again of what the old witch had said of the place she was headed. *The place of answers that breed questions, the place of truths that breed lies, the place of telling and finding.* Seris despised riddles and allegory. She preferred those who were straightforward and spoke plainly, but she could feel truth in the old woman's words.

Truth, and a promise.

Checking her navigator dial, Seris made certain she still headed east. She imagined what she would find when she reached her destination. What answers might finally be hers. As a youth, she had sometimes imagined herself as a child of the great ones, or a royal orphan. Especially when the other children were being particularly cruel. Of course, she could simply be the progeny of off-worlders as they had claimed, but she refused to believe such an origin for herself.

She remembered the day when her mother had finally admitted she was a mere foundling. That the people she thought of as her parents were actually strangers. Though she had suspected as much for most of her short life, the revelation had still stunned her. Seris had screamed at her mother that she was lying, that she was only being cruel like the others. But her mother had merely looked at her sadly, with tears streaming down her face, saying over and over, "I'm sorry, Seris, I'm sorry. I never thought to hurt you. I only wanted a child to raise."

"More like an extra pair of working hands," Seris had accused.

She'd left home that night and had never returned.

Seris shrugged, pushing the memory away. It had been many years since that day. She wanted to believe she had come to terms with who she was since that time, but Seris's longing for connection had never fully left her. Even among the outcasts who worked as mercenaries, she had never felt a sense of belonging. Her solo march into the desolation was a sure sign that nothing had changed. She had always been, would always be, an outsider.

The suns drew lower and the sky took on a dull slate color. Behind her, the distant mountains turned a deep red, disappearing slowly into the night. If not for the stars that filled the sky, the horizon would have been indistinguishable. The starry sky outlined the mountain tops, creating the illusion of a piece of torn beaded fabric with frayed edges hanging half way down a darkened wall. Seris realized the corner of her mouth had turned up in a half-smile as she walked relishing the beauty of the night. If not for her ragged thirst and the way her dried lips cracked with the movement, she could have enjoyed this moment. She shook her head slowly and shivered in the chill desert air.

She stopped, peering into the deepening darkness. There was no shelter to be had here, but she was tired and there was no point in stumbling on through the dark. She dropped her pack roughly on the ground. Sitting down beside it, she pulled out a small bit of the thin traveler's bread she'd brought with her. She sat there, chewing slowly. The dry ration felt and tasted like sand in her parched mouth and she had to force herself to swallow it.

The Desolation was aptly named. There was nothing for hundreds of kilometers in any direction.

The night chilled quickly, and she reached inside her pack, pulled out her extra tunic and overshirt, and put them both on. Then she unrolled her worn and weathered blanket and wrapped it about her.

Leaning back against her nearly empty pack, she sat staring up at the stars gleaming brightly above her. She knew their names and the names of the constellations they formed. She had learned them as a child. There above the horizon was Ruma, the Wanderer, and the Cluster of Hamos. To the north blinked Kindola, the Traveler's Guide who's bow always pointed south, the tip of her arrow glowing red as fresh blood.

Seris breathed in the cool night air, filling her lungs. Holding her breath for the visioning ritual before exhaling, she sat up and made the sign of the Way. Reaching up, then out to the sides, her arms straight, palms up, then bringing her arms in and crossing her wrists in front of her, she rested her palms on her chest. Closing her eyes, she continued the ritual breathing, counting her breaths. But, as usual, no visions came to her.

After a while she stopped trying. She sighed at her own stupidity. Why did she continue trying when she knew it was fruitless? She was a rarity, completely ungifted, why couldn't she accept that? She sighed again, audibly. It had been hard enough for her, being so different from everyone else physically, her gray eyes and ebony hair standing out wherever she went. But the lack of a gift had been worse. Most everyone on Kalan was gifted, at least in some minor way. Even people of average intelligence could at least sense, but Seris had no gifting. She had no acuity of sense, no talent with plant or animal. Nothing.

She leaned back once more and closed her eyes. Reaching down, she pushed a button on her weapon and a low humming started, growing higher in pitch until it passed out of hearing. Not that there's much in the way of wildlife out here, she thought, but better prepared than ambushed. With her strike blaster set on discovery, she would be warned of anything larger than a miser bug that might approach. Hopefully, anything smaller would be harmless. She pulled the blanket close around her and slowly drifted off to sleep.

* * *

Seris awoke, shivering, tugging at her blanket trying to tuck herself further into the small folds of warmth it offered. The Triplets, three satellites that circled the southern hemisphere of the night sky at this time of year, were visible high overhead, casting a hazy blue light down over the open plain. She sat up and rubbed her arms and legs with short rapid movements trying to warm herself, wishing for something she could use to build a fire. At least it would be morning soon. Then the desert would warm up again in the light of the two full suns.

She didn't go back to sleep. Instead, she sat staring out at the wasted plains bathed in the bluish, eerie light. There was something familiar about the way the ground seemed to glow. Something that nagged at her, like the answer to a question that can't quite be pulled into conscious memory.

The sky slowly eased from black to blue and then to pale violet as the first sun crept up behind her. The warming air smelled of sun-bleached sand. Reaching down, she took her weapon off sensor mode. No sense in wasting power. The map she carried was not only old but, like most, incomplete. There was no way of knowing how much farther she would have to travel before reaching her destination.

She stood up, dropping her blanket, then arched her back and stretched her arms and legs to get the blood circulating. As she leaned down to pick up the discarded blanket, something caught her eye. She froze for a moment, watching the shadow that shifted in the distance, a tiny speck that caught the light in places then disappeared again into the dim haze of morning.

Cautiously, Seris moved to a crouching position. Reaching into a side pocket on her pack, she pulled out her viewscope, switched it on and held it up to her eye. The scope's power was low, but enough. Seris inhaled and exhaled slowly. A new hope arose in her as she watched the object come into view. A bubbling spring, the sun's light glinting off the ripples as they broke the surface tension of the small fluid pond surrounding it.

Life-saving water.

Seris breathed more freely as she switched off the scope and tucked it back into her pack. She quickly wadded her blanket, stuffing it into her pack and set off in the direction of the spring, forcing herself not to run across the sloping dunes. Sand shifted under her and she skidded on the shifting surface, but kept her feet. The small spring came into view as she drew near, sparse green-gray plants clung to the banks of the small pool. No other signs of life were visible.

She slowed her pace and searched the horizon. Nothing.

If wild animals used this waterhole, they should be here now in the early lighted hours. Unless the denizens of this deep desert watered only at dusk. Or during the night. She scanned the surrounding area for tracks. The sands appeared smooth and undisturbed. Likely the result of the recent sandstorm, but still there should be some recent animal sign. Unless even the animals were smart enough not to travel this far out into the desolate waste. Or had another reason not to drink.

Cautiously, she approached the pool. The plant life clung on tenaciously. There was little to no soil apparent, which could account for the sickly hue of the vegetation. Still, the water itself could be the cause.

She sank to her knees beside the pool and slipped her pack from her shoulders, opening a small pocket and removing her minerals kit. With a practiced precision, she dipped a vial into the water, careful to collect the sample from just below the surface. Her movements deft and quick, she added one chemical and then the next, holding the vial up to the morning light and watching for any change in color.

The final testing complete, she leaned forward and cupped her hand, bringing the water to her lips and drinking deeply. Too late, she realized her mistake.

The tingling sensation hit her tongue first and then seeped into her lips.

Curse her old gear! But chemical updates were expensive, and came with short expiration dates, and she'd had to make hard choices since leaving her last merc posting.

She fell back, away from the pool, letting the remaining water spill from her hand and spatter onto the white sand. Her numb fingers crawled toward her pack, reaching for the air powered syringe she kept for emergencies.

* * *

She lay on her back. High overhead, the first sun glared harshly as the second cast its morning rays across the dunes. She tried once more to wiggle her fingers. The numbness sat heavily on her, as if she were buried beneath a pile of rubble.

Funny how she'd never noticed before the way the sky's coloring turned from the morning's deep magenta, then faded to pink before becoming the pale purple of day.

The sound started as a far-off buzzing, like an angry swarm of insects. The humming grew louder. Sand skimmers. Her mind registered the danger, her heart attempting to beat faster despite the drug that flowed through her veins.

The buzzing grew close, then ceased.

Footsteps.

A wide shadow fell over her.

"The day's catch," a deep voice said.

"A bit scrawny, if you ask me." A second voice, farther away. Also male.

"As Mother always says, beggars can't be choosers, Gar." The first man leaned over her. "Let's get a better look." He pulled her eye shields up, exposing her face.

Her lids fluttered open, just enough to see his features through her lashes. Unshaven jowl, bent nose. He'd probably seen more bar brawls than the average mercenary.

"The old hag was right," Bent-nose said. "She'll do fine for the lesser brothels, or the mines." He grabbed Seris by the wrist and heaved her into a dead man's carry.

"Careful," said the one named Gar. "You know how Mother Vasquin hates bruised goods going up on the block."

"Shut up," her captor grumbled. "There's more than bruises on this one before we turn her in." He let out an ugly laugh as he tossed her onto a ratty blanket.

He let out a howl as the first blast hit him in the thigh, just below his crotch. He fell back, clutching his leg, and stumbled into the shallow pool with a splash. Seris didn't wait to see if she'd struck his femoral artery.

"You Afresian bitch!" Gar rushed across the sand, lunging at her.

She only had an instant to turn the blaster and pull the trigger. The bolt of energy seared a hole in his chest. A stunned look crossed his face as he crumpled into a heap. The smell of burned flesh wafted on the air.

Bent-nose growled. "You killed him." Blood poured from the wound in his thigh as he crawled out of the water. "How the hell?"

"Toss your weapon to me." She pointed the blaster at him. "I've got another good charge or two on this." She held the weapon so he couldn't see the blinking power cell light.

His lip curled as he reached for his blaster.

She gave him her most dangerous grin. "Slowly."

He tossed the weapon over and she grabbed it, dropping her own. "You are not only stupid, you're gullible."

He lurched toward her, but his wounded leg bent under him uselessly, blood still pouring from the wound.

"I'd put some pressure on that," Seris told him. "For what it's worth." She picked up her syringe and eyed it before tucking it back into the emergency pocket of her pack. No sense wasting the remaining dose of serum. Luckily, the two miscreants had arrived when they had. Much sooner and . . .

She kicked over Gar's body, just to be sure. Then plucked his weapon from its holster. She'd never liked killing for pay, but this? But the realization hit her how different this was. The deaths of these two wouldn't keep her up a single night.

She inspected the sand skimmers. "Tell me," she said, as she stripped everything of value from the older vehicle and packed it all onto the other. "How much is true?"

She found a water tube strapped to the vehicle, drained it and wiped her mouth with the back of her hand.

"What?" Gar asked, attempting to wrap his belt around his thigh just above the bloody wound, his hands fumbling awkwardly on the buckle.

"How much?" she demanded. "How much of the story is true and how much the fortune teller's twisted lies, spun to herd lost souls out here to be captured and abused by you and that pile of crap you called Gar?"

"Watch your mouth. That pile of crap was my brother!" he yelled, yanking the belt tight to stanch the flow of blood.

Seris shook her head and pointed the blaster at his chest. "How much?"

"You're as misguided as the rest of them." He laughed, then grimaced in pain at the movement it caused. "No need to make anything up. There are always stories. And there are always fools who will believe."

"Who's the bigger fool?" she asked. "The person who believes there might be something in this world beyond knowing? Or the man so focused on his crotch that he doesn't disarm a captive before attempting to rape her?"

He tried to spit at her, but his mouth didn't quite work anymore and only succeeded in sending a line of drool down his own chin.

She set the self-destruct timer on Gar's blaster and strapped it to the empty skimmer. Despite the drugged water that had made its way into his system through his open wound and the loss of so much blood, there was no reason to take any chances.

"Mother is not going to be happy about this." His voice slurred.

"You're right about that," Seris agreed, straddling the loaded skimmer and switching on the power unit. She sped off, heading back across the desert waste. Behind her, the sound of an explosion reverberated across the barren sands.

"Not happy at all."

J.A. Giunta

Joe is a Fantasy author with numerous short stories and books published in both paperback and eBook. He has a B.A. in English from Arizona State and has worked in the IT industry for over 15 years. He now writes novels full-time at home.

He lives with his wife, Lori, and daughter, Ada Rose, in the perpetual summer that is central Arizona.

On the Web: jagiunta.com

RELATIVE
by
J.A. Giunta

Francis stepped out from the sandwich shop and into the autumn cool of a sun strewn courtyard. Between tall glass buildings, its center fountain was a work of art that misted the unwary and set loose rainbow light in colored stains across the air. Comfortable benches of smoothed stone formed a wide circle all around it, while others had been placed beside potted trees and bronze statues for the shade they offered.

Most of those seated to enjoy lunch, like Francis, wore business casual. Though acquainted with a few, he chose a bench off to the far side, away from the trail of busied footsteps and forced hellos. The scent of fresh cut grass was a welcomed bitter that kept at bay the cloud of perfume and smoke that seemed to have taken root in the cement.

He took a seat with audible relief, stretched feet and toes within their shoes and took a glance at his watch, always mindful of the time. He sipped his coffee and looked out at cars passing beyond the grass, as if the sound of their disappearing into the distance eased his mind.

When he finally reached to unwrap his sandwich, he felt the intrusion of her approach before she had even said a word.

"Mind if I sit here?" she asked.

She was pretty by any standard, with the confidence that comes with it, clean and well dressed, but far too young for even flirting. She may have been to college, but to Francis she looked a child.

He gave a polite smile and held up his left hand, so she could clearly see his wedding ring, and took a bite of sandwich without so much as a second look.

Her surprise turned to revulsion.

"What? Eww, no," she said. "I just want to talk."

He tried not to take the remark personally. After all, he wasn't interested in her either. He began to wonder what she was selling when she misconstrued his silence for approval and took a seat.

"You're going to find this hard to believe," she went on with little pause, "but I'm your granddaughter."

Francis laughed and nearly choked on a bite of sandwich at what had to be the strangest line he'd ever heard. She looked back at him deadpan.

"Oh, you're serious," he said. "Look, you're attractive and all, but I'm just not interested."

A frown marred her brow.

"What's gotten into you today?" She took the paper napkin from his sandwich wrapper and handed it to him, just as a piece of tuna fell onto his shirt. "No, seriously, you're my grandfather on my mother's side, and sometimes I travel back to this day just to talk." As he struggled to clean the mayo from his shirt, she added, "You're a good listener, and there's none of the emotional crap on

22

your part, because you never really believe me anyway."

He tossed the napkin into the trash.

"What's your name?"

"It's Joyce." She waved him off before he could speak. "I know, you're Francis, even though mom always says it's Frank."

His eyes had lit up for a brief moment. "My mom's name is Joyce."

"I know. Technically, it's Joceline," she said and tossed her hair back with a shake, "but, yeah."

He began to wonder if he was being filmed. A quick look at his watch showed he still had plenty of time, and part of him was eager to indulge this girl's delusion—or go along with the silly prank for the fun of it.

"Alright, I'll play." He turned to face her and took a drink of coffee. "So, people in the future can just travel back whenever they want, do whatever they want, without worrying about consequences?" Francis sounded dubious. "Doesn't sound like the government I know."

"Not just anyone," Joyce replied, a bit defensive. "Only a small percentage of the population can manage it, but travel isn't something you can stop, no more than I could stop you from thinking about grandma Jen or cutting out of work early today to surprise her with the dinner reservation you made last week." His look of mirth slowly turned to one of concern, and he began to wonder if she was a stalker. Not that she noticed or even slowed. "It's a mental thing, like meditation. There's no machines or drugs or technology. And you can't change the past. It's already happened."

"But you're here," he argued, "supposedly before you were born. How's that possible?"

"Time isn't linear," she said with a shrug. "It's as simple as that, and once you can get your head around it, really and truly understand it, travel becomes possible."

Was he really buying any of this? The way she spoke with her hands, that shake of her hair now and then . . . it reminded him of Jen. But that could be on purpose, part of the prank. It just didn't feel that way. She seemed to *believe* what she was saying.

"Why me?" he asked, eyes narrowed. "Why today?"

"You, because mom loves you so much," Joyce said and smiled, "talks about you as if you were the greatest man that ever lived." She had a faraway look in her eye and shook it away. "I get that. And today, because it's the day that broke mom's heart but also the day she decided to have me. Or so she's told me."

Francis gave half a smirk. "Ahh, so I die today. Don't suppose it's this sandwich? I always knew tuna would kill me."

Joyce laughed at that. He was surprised at how much he enjoyed to hear it, how it reminded him of his daughter. It was a ridiculous notion, but what if she was telling the truth?

"Why in the world would you come back to tell me I'm going to die?"

"I didn't!" She rolled her eyes and teased, "That is so typical of your generation. I came back to talk. You know, about *my* problems."

He couldn't help but chuckle.

24

"I think mine might be a little more pressing," he said, "given the circumstances."

"Yes, but I can't help yours. You can help mine. Or at least help me help myself."

Francis put his sandwich away, suddenly no longer hungry.

"Just seems strange you'd tell me that."

She gave a sympathetic nod but looked like one who'd had this conversation a dozen times already.

"Sometimes I do, sometimes I don't." She looked as if she wanted to touch his hand but refrained. "It's just that every time I do, the conversation goes much better. Like, you give up trying to believe and just go along with trying to help me instead."

It was his turn to shake his head. He didn't know what he believed, but he could at least listen.

"Alright, well, what can I do for you?"

Someone approached from across the grass, a young guy in his twenties. He looked more a student than anyone who worked there—even the guys from IT. Francis assumed he knew Joyce, which would have pretty much blown her prank. The guy's smile grew wider the closer he drew near.

"Hi," he said to Joyce. "What is this place?"

It was clear in that moment when he addressed her that she was shocked by his attention. She swallowed hard and looked around, as if suddenly angry and afraid.

"Who the hell are you?" she demanded.

Taken aback by her tone, now himself afraid, the guy looked back the way he'd come, as if he thought to run like a scared child.

Joyce went on angrily, "And don't tell me you don't know what I'm talking about." He looked on the verge of tears. Francis thought maybe the guy had a learning disability and had gotten away from his caretaker. It would explain his demeanor, but Joyce was having none of it. Sternly, she said to him, "You don't belong here."

The guy turned and quickly walked away without looking back. Joyce moved to chase after, but Francis touched her arm. Not to hold her back, but as if to say the confrontation just wasn't worth it. Still, he could see how strongly she'd been affected.

"I don't understand," he said. "What's the problem?"

"I've come to see you literally hundreds of times," she explained. "He's never been here before."

"What's the big deal? I thought you can't change the past."

"You can't," she said. "So either he's always been here—" her tone indicated the unlikelihood of that— "or there's something wrong with me."

Francis looked at his watch. Time was running short.

"You say the past can't be changed." He thought getting her back on track might take her mind from the strange encounter. "So, it couldn't hurt to tell me how I die today."

She took a breath, slightly calmer, but still tried to see where the poor guy had gone off to.

"No, I've told you dozens of times before," she said, "and nothing's ever different when I come back."

"That you've noticed," he pointed out. "Small things might be different. Even if the past can't be changed, we're clearly not having the same conversation over and over, or else you wouldn't bother to come back."

"That's just it though," she said, "I'm not actually here. I'm interacting with you in my mind, not your physical environment."

He looked doubtful and poked her arm.

Joyce groaned her frustration. "I know, I know. It's just how your mind chooses to perceive me."

"Even if that was the case," he said, "just talking to me must cause some kind of change."

"Not for me," she said with a shake of her head. "A new timeline is spawned as soon as I arrive."

If she's not actually here, how did that guy see her? Francis wondered and looked to see if he was still around. *Wait, do I actually believe her?* He chuckled inwardly but considered it all the same. *What if he was like her, a time traveler? But then he'd be in* her *head, not mine. Right?*

He began to feel a twinge behind his left eye.

"So you can't change *your* past," Francis said, "but you *can* change my future." Her look seemed to say it was possible but that it didn't really matter – not to her. He imagined she might have tried to warn him a number of times before but had grown disheartened at never seeing any change. "Are there a lot then, people like you, from your time?"

She raised her brows as she considered.

"There's 12.7 billion people," she said, "but less than a tenth of a percent test high enough to qualify for training. Even then, few can afford it."

Francis found himself wanting to care about her, to believe. She did have some striking similarities to his wife and daughter. The feeling grew the more they spoke, despite how silly it all seemed. It was like waiting for the punchline that never came and secretly hoping it never would.

More than that, he didn't just want to help her with whatever problem she'd come to talk about. He wanted to see her smile again.

"What's it like?" he asked. "Are you happy?"

She sighed with a half-smile and gave a nod. "For the most part. Life kind of depends on where you live. In the NA and Europe, things are much better than they are in, say, Asia or Africa."

That's not surprising, he thought.

"And what do you do?"

"I'm a processor for the largest BE on the west coast." She'd already begun to answer before he could open his mouth to ask. "Banking Entity. Technically, I belong to the government, but they lease me out for quarterly terms. Yes, belong. No, not like indentured servitude." She seemed to know what he was going to ask before he did. "More like joining the military, except better. I got into some trouble with credit debt when I was younger and decided to sign a work contract. They provide housing, food and a good paying job. I don't have a single expense, and when I get out, my debt is paid off. I even get to keep five percent of my total earnings."

"When you get out?" he nearly laughed. "Sounds more like prison."

"I meant get out of my contract," she said with the tired wrinkle of the mouth that all youth use to explain technology to their elders, "and trust me, you wouldn't compare it to prison if you knew what they were like."

Francis tried to imagine how incarceration could be any worse.

"OK, well—"

"What's a processor?" she finished for him. "No, it's not like data entry. I'm part of an MPU. A multiple processing unit." He was getting tired of having his questions answered before he could ask them and began to wonder if she could somehow read his thoughts. "Basically, I go to sleep in a comfortable chair for twelve hours a day, and they use my brain for computations. Being a traveler makes me highly desirable for that sort of thing. Spatial acuity and all that."

He took a moment to try and grasp how that might all work, using someone's brain as a computer, but chalked it up to futuristic tech he probably wouldn't want to understand.

"So, if you've come to see me before" he said, in an attempt to sway the conversation, "to talk about all the problems in your life, what did you come to talk about today?"

She was quiet a few moments, as if unsure she wanted to bring up the real reason.

At last she said, "Dal and I just found out we're pregnant."

Francis' eyes went wide with a genuine smile, one almost born of pride.

"Congratulations! That's good news. Right?"

"Sort of." Her uncertainty tugged at his heart. "See, we're both under contract; we met at

29

our lodging compound. When a baby is born under contract, the baby automatically enters into their own contract, which lasts until they're 18." He could see the worry in her eyes, hear it in her voice. "We're only there for another two and a half years. We could extend for the duration, to stay with the baby . . ."

"Or?"

"Or we can opt out of our contract," she replied, "before the baby's born, forego all compensation and owe for expenses accrued during our stay. We'd have no jobs and a mountain of debt."

There was more than worry to her demeanor now. She was afraid. Was there a downside to the job she wasn't saying?

"If you don't mind working for, err, belonging to the government, then why—"

"Because it's different for a child!" she said, near to tears. "Their education, rec time, friends, their entire upbringing is designed to make them *want* to stay." Her eyes were pleading with him to understand. "We'll have to spend the rest of our lives in a lodging compound, or we'll never see him again."

As much as he wanted to remain distant from the situation, to offer his opinion as if she were a stranger, a part of him couldn't help but think of the unborn child as family. It didn't mean he believed her, but the thought of losing a child hit close to home.

"What does your gut tell you to do?"

"To run," she said in a trembling voice. "I don't mind my contract, because it's kind of nice short-term. I'm already grown. They can't change who I am. I just don't think it's the right environment for a child. Kids raised in restricted housing . . . aren't like other people."

"And Dal," Francis asked, "what does he think of all this?"

"He wants to stay." She said nothing of it, but he could hear the sense of betrayal in her words. "He's afraid we won't be able to find work, and we'll either starve or end up in prison when we can't pay our bills." She clenched a fist and shook her head. "I almost wish I could go back and talk myself out of signing. Then none of this would've happened."

Francis offered, "You wouldn't have a baby on the way, either." He considered. "Can you? Go back and talk to yourself?"

"Yes. It doesn't matter, though," she said. "You can't change the past, and I'm never very . . . helpful."

He could see gentle understanding just wasn't going to cut it. She was so much like his Gwen.

"Maybe you're not trying hard enough." He held up a hand to stop her protest, to let him speak until he was done. "Maybe, you already changed the past and don't realize it. Either way, that's not why you're here. You already made up your mind, and you want me to tell you it's okay. Sorry, but I can't do that. It's a shitty situation for sure, and no one is ever really ready to be a parent. But you do the best you can, you tackle problems as they come and you move forward, together, as a family. What you don't do is base life decisions on what may or may not happen. You can plan for the worst, make educated guesses as to how things might go, but you have to be willing to at least try."

31

Joyce began to cry.

"It's not that simple!"

"Life's never going to be simple," he said, comforting but stern. "It's a series of hard choices with some happiness and heartache in between. Everyone has problems; everyone gets scared. It's what you do with that fear that counts, what makes you who you are. So, what kind of person do you want to be? The type who gives up without even trying, who sacrifices the happiness of others for themselves? Or do you want to be the one who works hard, who does what it takes when things get tough, who puts loved ones first? Especially the ones who haven't been born yet."

She'd grown calmer as he spoke, as if soothed by his words and the care he gave his answer. She wiped her eyes with the back of a hand.

"That's a loaded question," she said. "I just want to be happy."

He tossed his coffee and sandwich into the waste bin. With a pat on her shoulder, he wished her luck and got up.

"Happiness is relative," he told her. "You're never going to find it by being afraid. What will you do?"

Joyce gave a nod, as if her mind was made up. "I'll opt out. Dal can stay if he wants. I won't let my baby be raised there."

"Good." Francis gave one last look at his watch. "If things ever get too hard, you can always come talk to me. Or, you know, even if things are going okay."

"Thanks," she said and smiled up at him. It warmed his heart to see it. He began to leave, to head back to work and whatever else lay ahead of him. "Frank," she called after. "Maybe take the bus home today? Save the environment and all that."

Francis smiled back. "I just might. Good luck with everything. I truly hope it works out for you."

"You too."

He was halfway to the glass doors when he looked back for a final glimpse, a last chance to see that smile, but she was already gone.

Scott Woods

Scott Woods is the author of We Over Here Now (2013, Brick Cave Books) and Urban Contemporary History Month (2016, Brick Cave Books) and has published and edited work in a variety of publications. He has been featured multiple times in national press, including multiple appearances on National Public Radio.

He was the President of Poetry Slam Inc. and MCs the Writers' Block Poetry Night, an open mic series in Columbus, Ohio. In April of 2006 he became the first poet to ever complete a 24-hour solo poetry reading, a feat he bested with six more annual 24-hour readings without repeating a single poem.

On the Web: scottwoodswrites.net

SECOND COMING SOON
by
Scott Woods

Harry Simpson looked down at the computer screen, his mouth covered by the thumb and index finger crook of his right hand. His email was packed with dozens of unread messages, which was a common enough headache, but this morning it was at least double what he was used to getting by this time of day. He stood up out of his chair and paced the space between his desk and the wall of glass overlooking downtown Hollywood, prepping himself for the rumors, bombs and pleas that would assault him once he started right-clicking his way through the pile of notes and RE:s. He looked at his watch. 10:14 AM. "This is gonna suck," he muttered.

He looked down at the headset intercom lying on his enormous glass-topped desk. He knew he couldn't avoid its lobe-clutching catcall forever, wouldn't be able to avoid his clients or their hordes of handlers the entire day. He knew he was going to have to don the plastic device and do battle with agents and woo clients and keep the money and jobs coming in. Harry was the top acquisitions agent in the firm, even though he almost never left his office once he got there. He did most of his business by phone or email and took meetings on *his* time. He knew he couldn't keep the game on his peculiar terms forever—there was always some hot new ad firm around the corner with the latest software or a Viking crew of art school graduates with CD-ROM portfolios waiting to dethrone him—but while he was on top of the pile, he meant to run things his way. He didn't much like dealing with people in Hollywood, be they clients or co-workers. There was too much weirdness masquerading as humanity, he had told a restless prostitute with acting aspirations not two weeks ago, and he was looking for a way to get out of the game while he still had the clout to move into greener pastures.

The only holdup was that Harry wasn't sure what his next career move should be. The not knowing picked at the back of his neck and made his ears sweat like he was in an after-school detention his mother didn't know he was serving. He was exceptionally good at what he did, was a perfect ad man. He lied at will, could detect the lies of others with mutant-like capability, had a smile that could disarm a terrorist with bombs taped to his body and a note from Allah in his back pocket, and cared for the company of no one, thus holding no professional or personal allegiances. He had no real friends in California, and the friends he'd left back in Ohio seemed not to have noticed that he'd moved away years before, if his answering service was any fair indication. He didn't date—had to buy the affections of women despite his fair looks for a man in his early forties who smoked a pack of Salems a day—and hadn't bothered to play the political game all other businesses vying for entertainment dollars in Hollywood were notorious for. He was the "Great White Shark" who chewed away at his competition with every tooth in his mouth. Harry's original boss

36

had told him that before Harry replaced the quivering sap a year later. His second grade teacher, Mrs. Vest, had even called him "villainous" in the middle of an assembly for reciting EC horror comic book stories to his pew mates during school mass. He had looked at her with such venom in that moment that she had Father Druscoll paddle him in front of everyone on the spot until he cried. Everyone laughed at him and called him "Holy Butt Simpson" for years afterward. He always wanted to be able to go back and show her a thing or two about actual villainy now that he had a Hollywood attitude and a Platinum card, but he'd heard she'd died while he was in college.

Harry sat in his swivel chair and reached for the pack of cigarettes in his pocket, not taking his eyes off the screen as he scanned the more notable names in the SENDER column and chalked up their relative importance to his existence: Roland Justice ("producer jack-off"), Tommy Squire ("mere idiot with rich uncle"), Pamela Reese ("drunk agent broad who can't keep her hands off her smarmy talent"), Harvey Goldberg ("filthy short-bus retard with ridiculous producer pretensions and a spitting slur"), James Warfield ("nigger"), Billy Diamond Jr. ("unfunny Napoleon complex-wielding nut with unrealistic Emmy aspirations"), Tom Creese ("pretty boy actor who needs a good sucker punch and a better plastic surgeon"), Harrison Williams ("no internal editor-having wop"). The list began to blur before his eyes, the idiotic agents' names swirling into the air-headed, personality-disemboweled actors' monikers. He pinched the bridge of his nose, wincing and sighing heavily. It was only eleven-something in the morning and it was already a long day.

"You should take something for those head-aches, Harry."

Harry shot up in his chair at the sound of the voice in his office. The sound hadn't been overly loud or scary. Harry thought it was actually pretty smooth, almost velvet-like. *It would have made great voice-over money,* he thought. *Wasn't the AV department looking for some new VO actors?* Harry instinctively reached for his business card case, his heart beating like a drum solo in his chest. Velvet or no velvet, there wasn't supposed to be any voice in his office but his. He looked around, twisting in his chair as he did, and found the voice's owner. Sitting under his original Ferjo on the Justin leather couch was a Black man wearing a long white pullover robe with a blue sash across his left shoulder that fell to his waist. Dreadlocks poured from the man's head like a fountain of ripe black cattails, and he sported a slim mustache and beard. His right leg was crossed over his left at the knees, showing sock-less feet in large leather san-dals that tied at the ankles. The man had a square jaw and an easy smile, but Harry couldn't stop looking into the intruder's eyes. They were a mag-nificent gold, and they seemed to both warm and warn Harry as he looked into them; kind of "How's it going, pal?" and "Can I borrow five dollars?" at the same time.

"Jesus," Harry huffed, rolling himself back toward the desk and shaking his head.

"Well," the stranger said, raising his eye-brows, seemingly impressed, "you're even faster than I'd heard."

"Look, buddy," Harry said, trying to find his stern voice through the fear. It was one thing to be interrupted, but a whole 'nother beast to have your office broken into by some homeless guy with ninja aspirations. "I don't know how you got past Glenda, but you got three seconds to get out of here before I call the cops."

The man smiled broadly and cocked his head to one side, looking Harry over. "Harry, that won't be necessary. This is a business meeting." Harry stiffened at the mention of his name again. He knew that any intruder might very well know whose office it was upon entering, but the sound of it coming from an unwanted stranger without socks on sent chills up his spine just the same.

"A business meeting, huh?"

"That's right." The man pointed at Harry's desk. "Check your appointment book."

Harry stared at the man while reaching for his leather planner, then looked down at the open page for the day. Just underneath the listing for his 10:35 phone call to Tom Hank's lead attorney and over his 12 o'clock work lunch with the stiffs from Graphic Design ("freak idiots with pens and T-squares") was the inked entry:

10:45 am – Meeting: Jesus

"I'm a little early," the man said.

Harry smirked at the sheet, closed the planner and looked up at the man.

"Okay, pal," he said, rising from his chair to walk in front of the desk, "who sent you? That piss-ant Caldwell? Wait, wait, June? Did my ex-wife send you up here? How much did you pay Glenda to change the book, so I can quote her the figure as I'm firing her ass?"

"I certainly hope you don't treat all of your clients like this, Harold. It can't be very endearing to them. Especially the actors. They're very sensitive, you know."

Harry sat on the edge of the desk and folded his arms in an attempt to make them look bigger as they squeezed against his flat chest. "Look, you do great work, but I don't have time to sit here and play games with you, pal, so let's go. Hit the bricks, Jesus. Least they could do was send a white guy. Come on."

The man on the couch stopped smiling at this and Harry got scared all over again. Jesus stood up from the couch and stepped toward Harry. The man stood at least a good three inches taller than Harry, and Harry was six feet. The executive's eyes danced around the office, trying to avoid staring into those golden, knowing eyes.

"Harold, I came here for your assistance. I am prepared to compensate you more than adequately for your work, but I won't waste time bickering with you. You either want my business or you don't."

Harry opened his mouth to berate the man again, but stopped. Something about the stranger's gaze filled him with . . . what? What was Harry feeling? It wasn't just fear, he'd known that on sight. Apprehension? Dread?

Opportunity. Harry's mental business sensors went off and he figured he'd entertain this for a minute to see where it'd go. The guy was a nut job, sure, but that didn't mean he couldn't learn something from him. Harry had turned all sorts of unlikely prospects into goldmines. Maybe this underdressed Rastafarian had something Harry could use: a line, a bit of slang that hadn't made it through the marketing grapevine yet, a keen outlook on sandals in October. Who knew?

"So let me make sure I got this straight," Harry started, "you're THE Jesus?"

"Yes."

"And you're Black?"

Jesus sighed and stepped closer to Harry's desk. "I knew this would be a tough sell before I got here. That's why I came to the top man on the advertising totem pole." Harry smirked at the compliment. "What you drinking there?" Jesus asked, pointing at the water bottle on the desk.

"Spring water. My doctor says I don't drink enough water."

"Well then it must be true," Jesus said, reaching for it. "You mind?"

"Mind what? You thirsty? We got a water cooler down the hall by the security desk." Jesus half-smiled at the hint.

"I just figured you'd want some sort of proof, is all."

"What are you going to do, turn the water to wine?"

"It's late enough for wine. How's a nice white sound?"

Harry chuckled. "While you're at it, why not make it a Hess Cabernet Sauvignon?"

Jesus looked at Harry, unblinking. "What year?"

"What else? '92."

Jesus waved his arm in one clean, quick motion, and then folded his fingers together, smiling. The contents of the bottle instantly went a rich gold and Harry leaped off of his desk.

"Jesus," Harry whispered.

"Exactly. Need more proof? Try this: remember that dog your mom bought you when you were eight? You brought him back home from the park one day and you were crying and holding him in your arms, and your mother asked you what happened to Kazaan and you said he got trapped in a sewer drain? Remember that?" Harry nodded, scared to blink. "I know you slid Kazaan down the sliding board over and over until the poor thing was shaking from shock and his little light just . . . went out."

Harry looked at the stranger—who was getting even stranger by the second—looked at the water bottle and back at the man who had to be Jesus.

"Well, now that we've got that all sorted out," Jesus said, seating himself in one of the chairs directly facing Harry's desk, "I guess we can get down to business."

"You . . . you're . . . what are you doing here?"

"Haven't you guessed? It's the Second Coming."

"You mean Judgment Day?"

"Not quite, but don't tell that to the Catholics. You know the Bible was always supposed to be something of a guidebook. It wasn't supposed to be taken so literally after all this time, you know? We figured—"

"We who?" Harry asked, holding a hand up to stop Jesus.

"Me and God. We'd hoped that you all would—"

"Wait a minute." Harry started pacing, rubbing his temples roughly. "I thought you were one and the same."

"Semantics, Harold. Man couldn't take a full-blown look into the face of God. Flesh isn't built to withstand that kind of exposure to actual holiness. Look, let's not get too wrapped up in this part. I'd really like to get to—"

"So if you're here, then it means that the world is about to end?"

"Well, not on this trip. That's not my goal here. This is sort of a set-up meeting."

"Set-up meeting?"

"To discuss my campaign."

"Campaign?"

Jesus stretched his fingers across his face, pulled down on his beard, and sighed. "Why else do you think I'd come here of all places, Harold? I need some down-to-earth advertising done on an international level and I've heard you're just the man to put it all together."

"What . . . what is it you're trying to say?"

Jesus straightened up in his chair, smiling at the question. He looked as if he'd been practicing this part in a mirror. He held his hands up in front of him, pulling them apart as he spoke. "Okay, Harold, get this: 'Coming Back Soon: The Son of God'. Lower caption, fade in: 'Are you ready?' Eh? What do you think?"

All fear and apprehension left Harry's body as he stared slack-jawed at Jesus. Harry's motors began running, clicking slogans against images and swirling backgrounds in his head. At the same time he managed to say, "That's horrible."

Jesus's smile faded and his hands dropped into his lap. "Well, what do you see? You're the expert."

"Well," Harry said, stepping to his own chair behind the desk, "I see any number of possibilities, but it all depends on what we're selling here."

"How's Everlasting Life grab you?" Jesus said, smirking and leaning back in his chair, putting an arm over the back.

"No good. Too determined. Have you taken a look around this dump of a planet? No offense,"

"None taken. I didn't make it."

"Okay, but most people are so utterly unhappy with their lives and devoid of anything smacking of imagination or dreams that the Everlasting Life pitch just sounds like they're going to be living the way they are, forever. That's no good. No, what you need is something that says, 'REWARD'."

"Reward."

"Yeah."

"Harold, Everlasting Life *is* a reward."

"Everlasting Life is a shampoo. What else have you got? Like, why are you here?"

Jesus perked up again. "I'm here for one last redemptive trek to get everyone who is willing to open their hearts to God's love ready to go when the actual Day of Judgment comes." Harold stared at Jesus blankly.

"Can't you just wave your hand and make people do what you need them to do? *Make* them believe?"

"Now, as always, Everlasting Life and Love must be gained through Free Will."

Harry shuddered at the words. "Free Will? You think I helped Oat Sensations move a million units of Crazy Wheat with Almonds because people felt they had a choice? You think that *Germinator 2* flick had a hundred mil opening because people felt they could *choose* to do something else that weekend?!" Harry chuckled. "No offense, but advertising agents don't believe in Free Will."

Jesus shot Harry a look that chilled the executive. "I'm not an advertising agent. I'm the Son of God."

"Okay, but we're dealing with some pretty scary demographics here if you're looking to sell something as nebulous as Eternal Life, which again, I think is a bad, bad pitch."

"Demographics? What do you mean?"

Harry bit his bottom lip, looking Jesus over, then asked, "Do you have to be Black when you come back?"

"Why?" Jesus asked, looking annoyed for the first time. "Is there a budget issue? Should I get some white background dancers for the traveling choir?"

"No, no. It's just a tougher sell to wider audiences if you're not white."

"Harold, whites are eleven percent of the world's population. I'm a world-class act, if you get my meaning."

"You think that makes a difference? Do you know who Michael Jackson is?"

"I'm not changing color."

Harry slumped back into his chair, drumming his fingertips together and frowning. "When were you thinking of launching this, anyway?"

"I don't think it's really appropriate for me to reveal that kind of information at this point."

"Look, J, I can't launch some campaign if I don't know what my window of opportunity is. You don't want to come back and start this world tour you're talking about the weekend that, say, the new *Harry Potter* movie comes out, do you? I mean, this takes a lot of math and precision planning to do right. I can't just . . . "

Harry stopped. It suddenly occurred to him that as of this moment, no one had said anything about what Harry was to get out of all of this. What was "more than adequate compensation" for his services? It was flattering that a figure like The Son of God might think highly enough of Harry's work to seek out his aid, but what exactly was He offering in return? Harry hadn't been to church since he was sixteen, and had skirted in recent years the notion of atheism anyway, so Jesus couldn't possibly expect Harry to do this *gratis pro Deo.* Just because Jesus Christ was sitting across from him didn't suddenly make him virtuous and Heaven-bound, just the top of the advertising food chain. Besides, what would he do in Heaven forever? If there was anything he could think of that could make him happy on Earth, he certainly had the money to buy it. There wasn't anything Harry couldn't get through one set of means or another right now. The misery of his personal life was clear and sharp, but it fueled him for what he truly savored: the thrill of the sell. He lived for the hunting of his enemies and their resultant professional demise. He dreamed of destroying any and all contenders to his advertising throne, and the many notches on his belt in this respect warmed him the way no rented or free woman could. Was there a place in Heaven for someone who feasted on the blood of his foes but did Jesus "a solid" once? Harry didn't think so.

"Just a second there," Harry said, pulling a pen out of a drawer in his desk while ripping a piece of paper out of a yellow pad in front of him. "Forgive my anxiousness, but we haven't covered something very important here."

"What's that?"

"Compensation. You're asking me to set up what will likely be the biggest thing since Barbara Streisand's third farewell concert, and for what? I don't know."

"Well," Jesus said, crossing his legs, "I figured that being guaranteed to pass into the gates of Heaven would be sufficient recompense. Plus expenses, of course."

"Yeah, well, I don't know," Harry said, scribbling some figures on the sheet. "See, these things cost money, number one, but there's a whole slew of things I have to arrange every time you get ready to make an appearance. There's venue clearance, insurance—which I don't mind telling you is a pain in the, well, you-know-what—rushing of the promos out to all of the major outlets, which by itself could break the financial back of almost any ad agency, no matter how good they are.

"Then you got security issues. I mean, yeah, you've been dead before, but what about the poor sap who crawls out of his deathbed to come see you and gets crushed by a mob of people who want to touch your robe? What if the gimp dies? You're talking major lawsuit. I know what you're thinking: 'Harry, I can just touch the guy and he'll be healed.' Well, near as I can tell, you only got two hands and I think the risk is a little greater than you may want to give credit for. Crowds are very tricky business.

"Then there's merchandising, agents, new phone system for the press traffic—"

"Wait a minute," Jesus interrupted, sitting up uncomfortably in his seat and re-crossing his legs the opposite way, "I have money, but that sounds like an awful lot of . . ."

"Carnage, J. Pure and simple carnage. You saw the Beatles, when they came over here and people were turning over buses—BUSES—just to see the look on their faces. Speaking of which, when you go international? Man, don't *even* get me started. I got three words for you: European soccer crowd. If they kill twelve people because some ambidextrous limey kicked a ball into a fishing net, what do you think's going to happen when the Son of God shows up at the stadium? And you'll have to do stadiums in the interest of public safety, which I'm sure you care about. No small venues at all. Every time you show up somewhere it's going to be pure carnage. Not chaos, my friend, *carnage.* So you understand why something that I'm not going to be able to bask in until I'm dead isn't very much incentive."

It was Jesus's turn to look at Harry in amazement, and they sat in silence for a full minute until Jesus let out a half-laugh of disbelief. "You know, when I came in here this morning, I knew this was going to be tough. You're Harold Simpson, best ad man in the country. 'Get him and you're as good as gold,' they said. I didn't think this would be easy. I *did*, however, figure that natural decency and common sense would prevail with you and that you might look at this as, not an opportunity for personal gain, but a chance to really bring the world into a new day. Into rapture! I mean, if you could just see, for one *second*, what Heaven was like . . . ah, well. What are streets of gold to a rich man, hmm?" Jesus rose from his chair and looked down at Harry with what the executive thought must have been pity, except he wasn't sure since no one had ever looked at him with pity to his face before. Harry set his pen down.

"Can I ask you something?" Harry said. "Hell, is it pretty bad? I mean, as bad as they say?"

"Oh, Harold," Jesus said, shaking his head slowly, "it's worse."

Harry bit his bottom lip. "And Heaven, it's really nice?"

"There are no words to describe its glory. Everyone there is in constant and everlasting bliss, savoring happiness without break or measure, save eternity."

"So . . . where did Mrs. Vest end up?"

Jesus frowned. "I'm sorry?"

"Mrs. Vest, you remember, my second grade teacher? The one who had me paddled in front of the whole school? Made my life hell, got me stuck with that nickname? Mrs.—"

"Vest, yes, I recall. She is in the open and saving hands of our Lord."

Harry looked up at the ceiling in thought, biting his lip some more. He seemed to be working out a math word problem in his head, seemed to decide on an answer, and reached into another drawer. He pulled out a thick, stapled thirty-page contract. Mrs. Vest had wanted to show the world his so-called villainy and it had made him a cold child and a bitter man. Harry figured he'd return her the favor in spades. Apparently, it was never too late for a little payback. *Besides*, he thought, *Great White sharks never sleep, do they? What was one more soul in Hell compared to a successful tour of The Son of God?*

"Okay, Jesus, I'll tell you my offer."

Colette Black

Author of our upcoming release, "Moon Shadows," Colette Black writes New Adult and Young Adult sci-fi and fantasy novels with kick-butt characters, lots of action, and always a touch of romance.

Colette was awarded the 2014 Howey Award for her sci-fi novel, "Noble Ark," and won the Coppercon 32 short story contest for "Kairos' Opportunity."

Colette lives in the far outskirts of Phoenix, Arizona with her family, two dogs, a mischievous cat and the occasional unwanted scorpion.

On the Web: coletteblack.net

SWAN'S PETITION
by
COLETTE BLACK

The true story concerning the unsubstantiated myth of "Zmey Gorynych and Dobryinya Nikitich," from the journal of Zmey Swon- -second son of the wind dragon, Swon Chao, and shapeshifter, Mila of Gorynych. Ukraine-Russ; 964 AD

Moonlight in my eyes, I waited in the strong arms of an old pine, hesitant, but hopeful. Occasionally, I shook the limbs around me, letting Zabava know where I could be found. Father would have been able to rustle those boughs at will, cooling his skin with a light breeze. He could have brought the gossip of the castle, anything spoken out of doors or near an open window within a hundred miles, to his waiting ears. But not I. Though seventeen years and a strong man of good wit, I'd shown no signs of becoming a wind dragon—able to flatter the wind to my whims like my father and siblings—nor a shapeshifter— changing shape to commune with animals like my mother and sister. Even my younger brother, Vuk, had started his wind-dragon training at twelve. No boys dared bother him with the wind enforcing his punch, making his feet fly faster, higher, and harder.

The flapping of Zabava's wings raised my eyes from the path to the sky. Her white feathers extended outward, silhouetted by a crescent moon, slowing her descent as hooked toes reached for a thick branch well below me. A ping of fear coursed through me. I'd seen her shift before, but never when I stood so close. Would she be clothed? Part of me hoped not while the better part of me chastised my wicked desires. I only had a moment to wonder as a huge, dark fabric extended over what little I could see of her body. When she emerged, she was fully clothed, including a hat of fine lynx and a knitted shawl. She climbed with the ease of a shapeshifter, able to draw on nearby animals to accentuate her abilities. Settling on a thick limb across from mine, her hands at my knees, she smiled.

"Still afraid of me?" she asked.

"I've never feared you, Zabava. You are my dearest friend."

She frowned at that. "You did fear me, and I saw you shudder as I landed. I know I am ugly when I shift, so I can't truly blame you."

My tone grew much too sincere for our bantering. "You are never ugly. Never." I shook off my serious nature, probably making her think I shivered again. "But I worry about you flying against the moonlight. You could be spotted."

Zabava's instant smile drew me close, like an insect to honey. "Pshah. Volodymir the Wolf doesn't care as long as I don't draw attention. No one notices a swan flying in the night."

"What if a hunter had seen you? He would shoot you for sport, not even for hunger."

She placed her hands on my knees. "And would you care?"

"Of course I would care." I drew her hands in mine. "I might never draw breath again if anything happened to you. You are the best of all my friends."

"Hmmph." She drew her hands away. "There's that word again."

"What word?" How had I offended her this time?

"What if I don't want to be your friend, Zmey?"

My heart seemed to beat from my chest then fall into my stomach. "I understand if you no longer wish to see me. I am a mere peasant, far below the consideration of a lady of Ukraine-Russ." I risked a momentary raise of my eyes, just enough to see her face so close, one last time. "Thank you for telling me in private."

"You're such a fool," said Zabava.

With the agility of the cat whose skin she wore, she bounded to her knees on the thick limb. "Do you think I coerced you to meet me, alone, in the middle of the night so I could tell you good-bye?"

She kissed me, long and deep. I fell backward. If not for her quick reflexes, it would have been the first, best, and last kiss of my life.

"Let's climb down from here," she said breathless.

I complied and we whispered of secrets, impossibilities, and plans, in between stolen kisses, until dawn threatened the horizon.

"We can never be together," I reminded her.

"Perhaps when you manifest, gain your God-powers, my father will concede."

I laughed, my voice thick with sarcasm. "I'll never manifest. You gained your powers at fourteen, Vuk at twelve. I'm seventeen. Even the gypsy woman said I don't have the power of the dragon or the power of the wind."

Zabava pulled back, gripping the sides of my shirt as if her small figure could throw me to the ground. "The gypsy is an ignorant charlatan. We of the God-powers are in a time of gathering, drawn to one another. I couldn't love you so much if you didn't have some gift from the gods."

Perhaps she didn't truly love me. And why should she?

I feigned heartbreak as a mask for my true anxiety. "And I thought your love was true, but it is only if I possess a God-power."

She swatted my arm, her laughter a balm to my fear. "Of course I love you, no matter what happens, but I still say you have powers. They're slow to manifest, but maybe you'll be a stronger dragon than most. I'd say shapeshifter, but . . . "

"I know. My mom can only shift into fish, and not very well. Still, I think you might have to accept that I'm an ordinary, with no inheritance of value. You would be better without me."

She answered by pressing her lips to mine. I didn't want to let her go, intoxicated by the smell of lilacs on her skin and the melodies of a peaceful forest.

"We will find a way," she said, before disappearing under her dark cloak, transforming, and then flying into the grey sky.

* * *

I kept a wary eye in the direction of Lord Putyatishna's manor as I used my bucket to pull water from the wide river. I don't remember the river's name, or if it had one, but I can still see the white foam in places where the current roiled around rocks above or near the surface. I can still smell the clean early-summer air, filled with the pollen of pine trees, the wind dusting the yellow-brown spores across my path. I wished Vuk was the one who had to haul water from the river to the growing crops, but I was the expendable one.

As I drew the water into the pail, I reached my mind toward the fish in the stream, like my mother and sister. My skin tingled, but like the hundreds of times I'd tried over the years, nothing happened. Father said it would come when I had the right motivation and my instincts led me to my power. I called to the wind, excited at the touch of a light breeze, until the breeze turned to a gust and I realized I'd had nothing to do with it.

Pollen fell like yellow rain, wind throwing dark strands of hair across my eyes. For the first time since Zabava and I had started stealing evenings together, I saw the full extent of her contorted resemblance to a whooper swan. I should have been at least somewhat repulsed, but I only set down my bucket and watched her descent with growing anticipation.

Webbed feet, connected to skeletal human legs, kicked up dirt and pebbles as she landed on the river's shore. Wings settling, her spindly legs filled out to womanly proportions. She quickly hid behind the wine-colored plumes of a smoke-tree bush, giving me a stern glare for watching, but how could I not? She was so beautiful. I only wished the recent rains had not been so generous and the bush hadn't filled out so completely.

As I gazed, the feathers of her immense wings disappeared, melding out of sight into supple arms. Her long neck shortened to normal proportions above her bare shoulders, and the flesh-colored monstrosity that vaguely resembled a beak formed back into her face, leaving full, perfect lips. Her pale skin, almost as white as the swan's feathers, accentuated the pinkness of those lips. Her long, blonde hair curved over her shoulders like a cascading waterfall to succulent lands unseen. She threw on a simple dress from the sack she'd strapped to her back then gobbled two enormous chunks of cheese and bread like a starving orphan. I was used to the voracious appetite of a shifter. My mother and the one sister to inherit her abilities ate like that after a change. And since we rarely had food to spare, they rarely shifted.

Before my admiration could make me lose all sense, I considered our surroundings. "Have you gone crazy? Flying in mid-afternoon, for all to see? King Volodymir could have you executed."

"Doesn't matter." Zabava's momentary smile slid from her face like her former beak. "That's why I came. There is a bogatyr here, Dobryinya Nikitich. He's headed to your home."

"The emperor's bogatyrs have come before, pumped up in their armor and conceit. They can prove nothing. Most believe as the villagers do, that we are Saracen, from the Muslim lands south. They hate us for it, but there's no real danger."

"Dobryinya knows your father comes from the East. He called you a Mongol. Your dark hair is straighter than the Saracen, and your skin is not as dark. He's not like the others, Zmey. He's clever, he's ruthless, and he's focused."

I kicked at the bucket, sending water over the edge and back to the river. "He can't suspect much. This is a land of shapeshifters and treemen, but even those with the God-powers believe dragons are legend."

"He has a tattoo, on the left side of his chest. It's a dragon with a sword through its belly. Didn't you say the man who chased your father from his home and killed his family wore such a tattoo?"

My hands clenched. "It can't be. He would travel so far?" Then realization hit like a stone in my stomach. "Why did you see him shirtless?"

Zabava blushed, heightening my sudden anger. "He asked me to bring towels to the bathhouse. When I went to leave them outside the inner door, he opened it, revealing himself."

My jaw clenched. "Did he . . . ?"

"I'm faster than that, Zmey." Her familiar grin returned. "You shouldn't have to question. Before the brute could lift his hand I'd apologized and stepped through the outer door. I accidentally smashed his fingers in the process." She chuckled. "Even a king's man doesn't dare run naked through the hallways chasing a lord's daughter, especially while crying about blood on his nails."

"Stay away from him," I warned.

She pulled something else from the sack she still carried. "I have an idea." In a small ornate cage, something designed for finches, slithered the strangest animal I'd ever seen.

"What vermin is that?"

"A three-headed sand-striper," said Zabava with a grin. "Stupid as firewood, but I think I could shift into it. If I can imitate the teeth and the glands, I might even be poisonous."

Reptiles were uncommon in our part of Ukraine-Russ. I stared at the thing in growing fascination. It had been years since I'd seen anything other than the occasional salamander or green tree jumper in the area around the farm.

"This Dobryinya is *that* dangerous?" I asked.

She set the cage down, giving me one of her firm stares "He is." She paused, seeming to gather her courage. "You should leave. You and your family. I will face him after you're safe."

I wrapped my arms around her, as I'd done so many times before, knowing I could be executed for touching a woman so far above my station. "I won't leave you."

She shook her head. "Until your powers manifest, there's nothing you can do. The man is a renowned warrior, one of the king's best, fearsome as the Knights of the West."

"I'll go warn my family," I said, "but I'm coming back. I have no secrets for the bogatyr to find, no reason to hide."

She bowed her head. "I'm engaged to a nobleman near Kyiv, to be wed as soon as I turn seventeen. It would be better for you to leave."

"We'll change your father's mind before that can happen. We agreed."

Zabava blushed, her pale cheeks turning pink as the delicate flowers mother planted outside our cottage. "I would run away with you, if you only ask." Her blush deepened.

"A last resort," I said. "I'll prove my worth and your father will accept me."

The look she gave me was a reminder of what we both knew might never happen. I was not only a peasant, but a powerless one. Another parting kiss, and I turned to leave, to find my family. Suddenly, a man pushed aside the tree branches in front of me.

"Dobryinya," whispered Zabava, voice weak.

The man entered the clearing at the bank, wiping a bloody sword on my mother's grease-stained apron, held in his other hand. "You are the son?" Dobryinya asked.

I nodded, my gut turning as though I'd dined on pig slop. So much blood. The bastard must have killed my entire family.

"This'll be easier than I expected," Dobryinya mocked. "One less wind dragon to pester the world."

I stared in shock, but Zabava stepped to the side, drawing Dobryinya's attention. "You think to frighten me, little shapeshifter?" He laughed, deep and cruel. "Your body isn't made for that kind of shift. Your familiar frightens me more than you do."

I turned, realizing Dobryinya was right. Zabava's attempt to shift into a three-headed lizard, like the one in her cage, was incomplete. Her natural familiars were avian, not reptile.

She'd grown scales across her mouth, hands, and feet, even developed claw-like fingers and toes. As I watched, her head elongated and she flicked a forked-tongue from between small sharp teeth. She hadn't changed in size and her attempt at duplicating the lizard's extra heads created only a

raised stub on one shoulder, like a hunchback—
monstrous, but not dangerous.

Dobryinya reached out, gripping Zabava's
arm. With a snap, her jagged teeth clamped onto
his meaty bicep.

"You hellish wench!"

He swung a fist, clipping her jaw.

"No!" I screamed.

Blood slid between her facial scales, yet she
held on. Using his free hand, Dobryinya pried his
arm free. Zabava staggered back, clutching her face
in both hands. No longer able to hold the shift, she
started to change back to full human, blood now
flowing from between her perfect lips.

I lunged toward Dobryinya, but stumbled.
Falling onto my face at the river's bank, I felt
nothing, not even the taste of grit.

Dobryinya grabbed her by the arms.

I struggled to intercede, pushing up on my
hands. My skin burned as if frying on a spit. "What
is happening?" The words sounded odd, a hiss.

"What have we here?" Dobryinya released
Zabava with a shove, turning to face me. "I was told
the son was a Dragon, like his father. Just another
shapeshifter?"

Shapeshifter?

"Zmey, run!" screamed Zabava. "You're not
ready for this."

Attempting to stand, I found myself on four
legs. They were covered in scales, the nails long
and curved, digging into the stream. Elation warred
with fear. Finally, a God-power, but as yet
unpracticed. How would I save Zabava?

I raised my head—heads, three of them—to
Dobryinya. There were three of him, too. How had

I done that? I strained, stepping back, tripping, then shaking my heads to separate the three viewpoints.

Dobryinya strutted forward. "You've managed the three lizard heads, but you're still no bigger than a birthed calf." He pulled his sword, stained in my family's blood. "And that's how I'll kill you. As I would butcher my dinner."

After all these years of waiting, hoping, preparing to be like my father and brother, and this is what I'd been given—the ability to change into a measly lizard!

My anger swelled like a hot fire in my belly. I fumed, my breath warming my feet. Feet that shifted farther and farther apart. I paused, in awe as I recognized the faint sounds of my own whisper, so similar to my father and brother. I'd memorized them, studied them, hoping that someday . . . but this was different. Instead of directing the wind outward, I was directing it in, warming it. And my now-reptilian skin stretched to accommodate. My physique enlarged, a tail elongating from my spine. I grew to the size of a horse, and then to that of the elephants from the East. I became more than shapeshifter or wind dragon.

The burning air churned in my stomach like a cyclone, making me nauseous and excited together. On instinct, all three heads snapped a large tree branch into pieces, devouring the wood. In the heat of the swirling wind inside my belly, the tinder turned to flame.

I stood tall, staring down at Dobryinya's pale face. "You wanted something more?" I asked, not sure how I spoke. "You wanted a dragon, Bogatyr Dobryinya, well now you have one."

I spit the mass from my belly. A number of burning twigs, some charred wood, and a ball of black smoke landed at Dobryinya's feet. The flames fizzled to nothing and the smoke dissipated in the breeze. If only I'd had time to practice.

He laughed, tightening his sword-grip. "I tracked your father from the Mongol lands in the east until I killed him here. You are a different dragon, but I will kill you just the same. My brothers and I will kill all like you."

"There are no others like me. Changes like this only happen once in a thousand years."

I thought of the man's vow, thought of the worry my father had carried my entire life, always looking over his shoulder, afraid to use his gift, afraid to be seen.

"Kill me," I said, "and your quest is finished. No more dragons of any kind. Otherwise, you die."

I could only hope that he would believe me. That if I didn't survive this, my brothers and others like him could finally find safety.

My left-most head snapped at his shoulder. In a perfect arc the sword split the air, severing my neck. A short, burning pain, and the head fell to my feet. It deflated, catching in the crevice of a rock. Small drops of blood dripped onto the pebbles then stopped.

Dobryinya laughed. "I'm sure one of those heads is the right one. I *will* kill you."

With my right-most head, I clamped sharp lizard-teeth round both legs, tasting warm blood. "You talk too much."

I shook him like an angry dog with a new-caught rabbit. Intent on burying his stinking face into the river's depths, washing away my family's stains along with his life, I turned. An unexpected swing blindsided me. Dobryinya had decapitated me again. He fell, along with the withering shell of flesh that had once been my second head.

This time, I screamed. A pain-filled roar sent plumes of smoke into the air. I'd thought my size would give me the advantage, but I was too clumsy, too inexperienced.

"Fly away, Zabava!" I yelled, though my voice remained oddly monotone. "Cry the swan's lament for me from your highest tower."

"I can't—" she cried.

"Trust me, and go."

She started to change, but didn't move. "But, I . . . I—"

"Go!"

She flew into the air. I wished I could do the same.

Before I could retreat, the sword arced again. There was still a slim chance for my survival. Zabava had said this bogatyr was clever, but he also seemed a vain glory monger. I focused, I whispered, I cowered and shrunk within myself, my world going black.

Dobryinya's sword sliced through scale and flesh. The pain staggered me. I dropped to my belly. A splash of something large landed in the river. My world was pain, darkness, and then all went still.

* * *

I awoke next to the stream, human, naked, and wishing to scream with the pain. Blood dripped into my eyes. I swiped it away and whimpered from the touch. Finding a spot in the water that afforded a less rippled reflection, I touched my face with more care. Part of my nose was gone, along with the flesh of my right cheek, part of my eyebrow, my temple, and a portion of my scalp. I was alive. I'd kept the illusion of the dragon head while pulling my flesh—most of it—back into the base of my neck, for all the good it would do me. With a disfigurement such as this, I would be a beggar for the rest of my life.

Still, I had to check on Zabava's safety.

After washing in the stream, I staggered to the closest farm, consumed a barrel's worth of apples, and then stole their oldest son's clothes where they hung on a post to dry. Hoping I wouldn't encounter Dobryinya again, I snuck back into the forest in hopes of finding a familiar that could fly. I attempted Zabava's swan, getting something similar after several tries. I couldn't stay off the ground long enough to go more than a few feet.

Zabava had made it look so easy, jumping into the air, gliding up on the currents, flying. But her elegant body was designed for air-travel, light and small-boned like her western mother, flowing and sensuous. I had taken after my mother as well—the sturdy build of the Slavs. I could grow feathers, and wings, but none of it would make me more than a land-bound chicken.

"Zmey?   You're   a   shapeshifter?" I spun to find the voice, Vuk's voice. "Brother? You're alive! I thought Dobryinya had killed all of you."

Vuk's face darkened, horror lighting his features as he saw the disfigured part of my face. "Father distracted him while the rest of us ran. I thought for sure the bogatyr would come after me next so I separated from the others, hoping to lead him away. In the next village, I heard talk of him killing a giant, three-headed dragon, supposedly the offspring of farmer Swon. I worried that the son of a whore had killed you then claimed more glory than he deserved."

"He did."

Vuk laughed then turned somber, touching a patch of raw skin from my forearm up to my bicep, avoiding close scrutiny of my face. "What happened?"

I told the entire story as Vuk's eyes grew wider. "That's impossible. We only inherit one of our parents' gifts, even in a Gathering, never both."

I shrugged. "I don't know how, but I am an exception."

"So you're a true dragon. Not just a wind dragon, but a real-to-life impersonation of the fantastic creatures drawn to represent us." He shook his head. "Amazing. You could rip that bogatyr into pieces, Zmey. Especially with my help."

I shook my head. "No. We kill him and one dragon-hunter is dead, but the rest will take it as a challenge. I told him I'm the last of my kind. You have only to stay unseen until Dobryinya leaves the castle. As long as you're careful with your powers, you'll be safe."

I could tell my resistance was hard for Vuk. I'd also wanted revenge for our father, but I wanted the hunting to end. He finally nodded. "It's what father would have wanted. He was a man of peace."

I flapped my wings, almost raising a few inches. "Now, if I could only find a way to fly, I could check on Zabava and be away from this place."

Vuk tugged at my left arm-turned-wing. "You'll never get off the ground the way you are. You're too disproportioned. Tell the wind to lift you, to make up for the weight."

"How? I don't under—"

"You've seen me do it a hundred times, brother." Vuk jumped into the air, spun like an arrow, and kicked the trunk at a point much higher than should have been physically possible. He jumped back and forth between the trunks like a child hopping rocks. When he finally landed, the air cushioned his fall so he raised no dust. "Whisper. Tell the air to support you. If you can fill a fake lizard-head with air, only losing a few patches of skin . . . " He pointed to another raw oval running from my jaw, along my neck, and past my collarbone. "You should certainly be able to manage flight."

It wasn't as easy as he claimed, but another thought came to mind. I grabbed Zabava's little cage she'd left behind, staring at the stupid lizard inside. At the same time, my senses reached for one of many bats hiding in the darkest parts of the forest.

"Hot air rises," I said, losing my feathers and replacing them with scales and membrane. I didn't puff up as big as I had when I'd fought Dobryinya, but I drew hot air into my body and enlarged my wings. "Take care of yourself, Vuk. Give mother and the family my love."

I thought Vuk's eyes watered, but with a swipe of his hand the moisture was gone. He set his jaw and raised his chin. "Have a good life. Hurry to Zabava before she gives up on you."

I nodded, took a running start, and lifted into the sky, a flying reptile bigger than any whooping swan ever seen in Ukraine-Russ.

* * *

Sitting in avian form at the top of her father's highest parapet, Zabava sobbed into her spindly knees.

I landed.

She screamed.

As I deflated and resumed my natural form, her stare turned to relief. "I thought . . . thought you'd died." She wrapped her arms around me, nearly toppling us from the building.

"Careful there," I said, grasping a protruding stone. "I can't actually fly, not without concentrating."

She pulled back, scrutinizing my face. I tried to duck away, but she lifted a delicate hand. "I'll go my own way," I said. "I just had to be sure of your safety."

"Well, I'm not safe. Not unless you take me away from here. Dobryinya can hardly walk.

He'll be fighting infection and pain from the poisonous bites we gave him for the rest of his miserable life. He's insisting on my hand in marriage as compensation for his wounds. My father bid me run to get away from the monster."

"By yourself?"

"I hoped not. There's a priest at a chapel west of here." She held up some scrolls. "You're one of the cleverest men I know. On the chance you survived, I had father draw up papers. The priest will marry us and keep the details private." In her

69

other hand she held a large pouch. "Father gave us money. We won't be rich as a lord or king, but we won't have to live the life of peasants, either."

I hugged her tight, relishing her lilac scent.

"Even disfigured and ugly, you would still wish me your husband?"

She kissed me, long and hard. "You're a hero. I love your battle scars nearly as much as I love you."

Arranging the knapsack over her wings and onto her thin back, I assured myself it was secure and not too heavy. The straps would break if I flew as a dragon with them. As graceful as a real bird, Zabava took off into the sky. With a whisper to the fresh evening air swirling around us, I followed, the first of the shift-dragons.

I, Sir Richard Swan, submit this translation to the Donum Council which oversees God-powers, on the twenty-third of June, year of our Lord 1665. I hereby beseech, on behalf of all Swon descendants, the council's assistance in curtailing the unacceptable murders by these sworn dragon-hunters, most especially Dobryinya Nikitich's descendants. They continue to perpetuate their father's spiteful mission, inflamed by revenge and prejudice. In return for the council's support, the Swon descendants agree to never again transform into the shape of dragons other than in the privacy of our own estates, secluded wilderness, or in defense of our families.

As a humble servant of justice, with rightful pleadings for assistance in this matter to end the Nikitich family's centuries of bloodshed and horror,

I await your response for the duration of four months, until the end of the month of October, year of our Lord 1665. After such time, we will be forced to take matters into our own hands.

    ~ Sir Richard Swan

Bob Nelson

In 1994, Bob co-founded <u>Anthology</u> magazine with writer <u>J.A. Giunta</u>. The magazine would run for ten years and print a wide variety of up and coming poets and writers. Also in 1994, Bob started the Essenzaslam Poetry Slam, which ran 13 years. In 1999, Bob founded Spokenworld.com, a pioneer internet radio station focusing on spoken word programming.

Currently, Bob is the chief of <u>Brick Cave Media</u>, a media microglomerate for the crazy ideas that he dreams up. In 2006, He released his second spoken word CD, Boboratory, available through the Brick Cave Media Store as either a physical CD or downloadable MP3's.

He serves on the Board of Anthology, Inc., and still occasionally wanders around the local poetry scene.

On the Web: boboratory.com

OUTPOST
by
Bob Nelson

Being in space is like being submerged in water. There is no sound, no movement. You feel a dull sensation that isn't noise, but isn't silence either. It's like you've been removed from existence, allowed to sit outside and stare in, and feel the continuous hum of life flow through you.

You can lose yourself in all that endlessness, all that . . . space.

Until you remember you have a job to do, and you turn your attention back to the task at hand. Something like a big hole ripped in the side of your ship by the laser cannon of a particularly angry Proximan battle cruiser.

My cruiser, the Earth Defense Navy vessel, the *Johnathan Reilley*—or as we called her, the *Jolly Jo*—sat beneath my magnetic boots, a mangled wreck.

"Captain," the voice in my helmet sounded strained, like all the voices of my crew. "If you can get to the auxiliary intake junction, we can cannibalize parts from that. It's point 3546 on the hull."

"Markiers, that's not going to happen." My head's up display put that point square in the center of the gaping hole I teetered on the edge of. "What else you got?"

We had been fighting the Proximans for days, and we'd taken a lot of casualties. So much so that all staff, including me, were currently working repair shifts.

"You'll need to come in for now, sir. You've already stayed out 30 minutes longer than your suit's max rating. We'll send Williams to the aft junction and take parts from the—"

Another voice broke in. "Captain, Jacks here. Just got word that reinforcements are 22 hours away. Command is asking for a status update."

"Jacks, advise command of our tactical situation. Send coded response level Alpha-Delta-Five. We remain battle worthy, and can fend for ourselves until reinforcements arrive." It was a lie, and a bad one at that.

"Captain?"

I inched my way back along the hull to the starboard aft hatch, magnetic boots scraping against scorched metal. "Would you rather we tell the universe we're an interstellar paper weight?"

"Yes, sir . . . I mean, no, sir . . . Will do," Jacks responded after a pause.

I climbed back into the airlock, waiting for the sweet return of air so I could take off the infernal helmet that came standard with the clunky, out-of-code XL2 suit. The hiss of the oxygen jets in the airlock was slower than normal. Not a good sign for the health of the ship and her crew. Even the most basic functions were failing. I stripped off my gear, dumping it on a stack of storage containers, then shoved the lock open and headed back to the bridge.

Normally, the bridge was my comfort zone. But in the aftermath of our most recent battle, there was no normalcy. The quiet chatter and occasional electronic chime had been replaced with urgent voices and a chorus of warning alerts from all over the room. Urgency drove crew members across the room from one panel to another, trying to salvage electronics before they burned out or otherwise failed. The elongated oval of the room was centered on the view screen at its front, and long banks of terminals were positioned around the walls. The command chair sat in the center, and above the terminals were a series of large portal windows that looked out into space.

Jolly Jo was the biggest Earth vessel assigned to this quadrant, but she was far from the biggest ship in the Navy. She was labelled a cruiser, but she was an older ship—not as tight or refined as the more compact cruisers commissioned into service lately.

I stood in the doorway for a moment, staring out at the chaos and feeling strangely disconnected, until a particularly loud warning klaxon brought me back to the moment. Catching my attention, nearby Commander Gertrude "Gerdie" Jacks leaned over to peer into an open console, assisted by one of the repair technicians. Seeing her response in this crisis reminded me again that I was lucky Gerdie had been overlooked by the more misogynistic and none-too-smart captains for being a woman, and not being from a military family. She understood command, despite her non-military background, and knew how to motivate people to get the job done.

I stepped into the center of the room and laid a hand on the headrest of the awkwardly tilting command chair. "Gerdie, I need an update on the primary system repairs."

"In a moment, Captain." She strained to reach down into the console as she spoke, far enough that she had to turn her head toward me to be able to reach her target. A grimace distorted her face as she manipulated something inside the guts of the console. Whatever she did must have been right, because the status monitors for the weapons systems flashed into life. On the wall above the console, lights flickered on and gauges surged.

"That should get us through." She extricated her arm from inside the system. "Go ahead and button her up, Evans. It's the best we can do right now."

"Damn." She held up her arm and a trickle of blood oozed across her wrist.

I snagged a clean work towel from one of the other damage control officers and tossed it to her. "Who knew a brat kid who stole hovercars for a living would end up saving Earth?"

"Who knew a flunky from officer school would defeat an entire Proximan squadron?" she retorted, dabbing at the cut. It was a shaky attempt at levity in an otherwise decaying situation. She smiled briefly, then reached over and grabbed her communications pad off the console.

"So far, we've managed to stop air leakage, and have sealed off the radiation-contaminated sections of the ship. I just got the weapons interface back online," she nodded in the direction of her completed work. "So, once we actually get the weapons back online, we should know if we have anything to defend ourselves with." She scrolled though some data on her comm pad. "Engineering says we have ten percent power, and no propulsion, yet. They are saying another couple hours to repair the broken exhaust cones. We don't have enough fuel to get anywhere, and the backup bridge says they've been in contact with *Bonne Home Richard* and *Misery*. Both ships are still 21-plus hours out. No sign of the remaining Proximan ship, but we know they haven't jumped yet, so they're here somewhere."

Bad and worse. I took it all in. I had to as captain. I had to be thinking two or three moves ahead, but none of our options looked good. "Do you need anything here? I'm heading to the engine room to see where else I can lend a hand."

She looked at me with that "leave me holding the bag" look she gave me when she was frustrated. She understood respect, and military protocol, but she also knew a pain in the butt when she saw it. She looked around, and sighed.

"No, we have all the hands we can use at the moment. When you get there, please let Engineer Baloth know we're ready to start tests on the rerouted command lines. All the internal conduits were fried and we had to reroute outside the ship."

"Serious?!"

"As a heart attack, which you have been providing ample opportunities for me to have these past couple days, thank you very much." She turned back toward the view screen.

I headed for the transport shaft. "What did I tell you when I recruited you?"

"Never a dull moment." She chuckled. "I thought you were hitting on me."

"Not my type." As the transport door closed, a towel flew toward me and I heard her say something about harassment.

Moments later I was in the engine room, standing in the midst of even more noise and chaos. Engineers and crew were rushing around putting out fires, both literally and figuratively. I found Chief Engineer Simmons scolding a young crew member, and I waited at a safe distance until he was done, noticing a stack of EMP mines in the corner of the room.

"Simmons . . ."

He turned, ready to unleash a barrage of orders at me, until he realized who I was. "Sorry, Captain, things are a little tough down here."

"It's okay, what can I do to help? But more importantly, why do you have a stack of EMP mines in engineering?"

He flashed a look over at them, then back at me. "Nowhere else to put them right now. Their storage room was taken over by medical."

Simmons put me to work on some damaged energy alternators. Having served in the engine room of another invincible class battlecruiser before making lieutenant, I knew these engines inside and out. As I worked, Simmons' voice rose over the din off and on as he shouted orders and berated the crew. After an hour or so, he approached my position and stared over my shoulder at the tangled remains of a badly fried transformer. I was up to my elbows in the damn thing, trying to tighten down a new diverter coupling.

"Captain," he said, "Commander Jacks needs you up top. If you're not done here, I can put—"

"I got it." I gave the connector one last turn. "It's done, Simmons." I stood up, handed him the sonic wrench, and pulled him aside. "Listen, go a little easy on everyone, okay? We don't any need stress-induced mistakes." He raised an eyebrow and I rested my hand on his shoulder. "It's gonna be okay. We're going to get out of this."

His face sagged and his demeanor changed. He was tired, too tired at this point. But all our lives depended on us being able to get the ship underway and show our enemies we weren't done yet. He looked like he might fall, and I braced myself to catch him, but he steadied himself, took a deep breath, and flashed me a smile.

"Aye, Captain," was all he said. He turned to start yelling at another poor crew member, but caught himself and walked with them instead. I made my way back up to the bridge.

Back on the bridge, things were less chaotic than when I had left, and waiting for me on the captain's chair sat a steaming cup of coffee.

"What's this?" I picked it up without waiting for an answer and took a drink. Right then, it was the most delicious cup of coffee I had ever had. Lost in my coffee, I didn't notice Jacks move up beside me.

"We can't give you a lot right now, Captain, but we can give you a hot cup of coffee." I sat in the chair and closed my eyes as Gerdie returned to her station. "Oh, and we can give you one-quarter ion power, too, but I thought you needed the coffee more, right now." She was facing the other way, but I could sense the smile on her face.

"Never a dull moment, indeed." I sipped my coffee. "Gerdie, let Sullivan and the rest of the officers know we'll be meeting in twenty . . . do we have an intact sit-rep room?" I shifted in the slanting command chair.

"We still have Conference Room Two, by engineering. No amenities online at the moment, but the room is still there."

"Good, let the senior staff know to meet in Conference Room Two. For any department with casualties to senior staff, advise them to send a representative, highest rank available. Evans, you have control." I stood up and Gerdie and I headed toward the transport shaft.

"Aye Captain." A visibly shaken Nikolai Evans looked up at us, the terror playing across his face. He was in charge of damage control and he was clearly out of his element taking command of the bridge.

I motioned to the view screen. "Watch that. If any bad guys show up, call me."

"Yes, sir."

As we stepped into the transport, Gerdie tapped away on her comm pad.

"Network up?"

"Yeah." She kept typing.

I pressed the transport lift code sequence for engineering. "Can we scrub oxygen yet?"

"Almost."

"Okay."

She looked up. "Okay what?"

"Just making mental notes for your next review."

She gave me a look that was half unsure if she should hit me or be worried, and went back to tapping. When the elevator slowed, she let the comm pad fall to her side and stared at the door.

"If I leave you in space, I'll never have to worry about another review." The door opened and she was moving before I had a chance to respond.

By the time I reached the conference room, Gerdie was already seated. Dr. Brighton was there, seated beside Simmons. The chief navigator Lieutenant Bill Jooth, weapons specialist Lieutenant Commander Jennifer Nurstrang, and pilot Lieutenant Jamie Cathers entered behind me and took their places. A moment later, Alex Menendez, head of security, and science officer Lieutenant JG Victor Abramova arrived. Was this all that remained of my senior staff? It was worse than I'd thought. My stomach clenched, but I put aside the guilt and grief. There would be time to mourn later. After we survived. If we survived. I noticed the Doctor favoring his arm.

"Doctor, let's have Ms. Jacks tend your arm while we talk." It was clear he hadn't had time to give his wound the needed attention. Gerdie was up and standing over the doctor before I finished. She reached for his portable medical kit before he had the chance to argue. The Doctor was our newest senior team member—we were developing a nasty habit of losing doctors in combat lately. I couldn't afford to lose another. Not this far out in the field.

"People, what's our status?" I turned to the table. In battle practiced precision, each department reported their status.

"We are working to assess our weapons status. We lost all electronic means of inventory and power level tracking. We are counting our missiles by hand, where we can get to them," reported Nurstrang.

Abramova deferred, as he had been coordinating damage control parties and had no real sciences feedback to provide.

"All decks have reported in. A complete sweep has been made." Menendez sat up. "As bad as things went, we did not pick up any nasties in that last attack."

"Do we know if they tried?" Lieutenant Jooth asked from across the table. "Intelligence reports say the Proximans have been increasing their use of boarding tactics in open space when in close combat with their enemies."

Menendez snorted. "The captain's battle plan had us moving pretty fast. The Proximans have used that strategy when ships are adopting more of the traditional stand-off maneuvers. If they had tried, the boarding party would have been left in space."

"Okay, Simmons." I took control. "Commander Jacks tells me that we have one-quarter ion and can move. Excellent work. What else?"

The chief engineer shifted uneasily in his seat. "Well, we've got power pretty much anywhere that hasn't been destroyed. I've got the scrubbers working again, so we have clean air."

Gerdie shot me an "I told you so" look from where she was finishing up dressing the doctor's arm.

"Like Commander Jacks says, we can move," Simmons continued. "Right now, that's all I know. We took a lot of damage, Captain, and we're about out of spare parts."

I turned to our chief weapons specialist. "Ms. Nurstrang, what do we have for weapons?"

She looked up from her comm pad. "First off, a big thanks to Ms. Jacks for getting the network back up." She nodded to Gerdie. "However, we have no energy weapons available. We haven't been able to do a full diagnostics to see if those weapons even work at this point. We still have some missiles. I don't have a count, but I would guess fewer than 50. And we have a good number of atomic warhead shells left. In other words, we have some rocks to throw. I'm just not sure if we have the ability to throw them."

I tilted my head, letting her words roll around in my mind. "Victor, do we have any indication of where the enemy is, or if they sustained damages?"

"Captain, I don't think it's a question of if they are damaged, but to what extent. Honestly, they could be sitting 3,000 meters off our bow, but with our sensors down, we have no way of knowing."

Gerdie spoke up, "Captain, I think it is safe to say that they have sustained some serious damage. Proximans don't let their adversaries live if they have a chance to kill them. If they were close enough to beat us with a stick, they would do so."

I had to be satisfied with that for now, there was nothing to gain by belaboring the point. We all knew we were sitting ducks in the middle of nowhere with a vicious enemy preparing to attack.

"Okay, we need to find a way to make a move. Mr. Jooth, I need a list of all neutral planets within ten hours' travel based on our current speed capabilities. Coordinate with engineering and make sure we have what fuel we need to get there and back in time to rendezvous with the *Richard* and *Misery* when they arrive. As per protocol, all our reinforcement ships will be maintaining radio silence and will not acknowledge us if we cannot be seen. Send the information on nearby systems to Commander Jacks as soon as you have it. This sector of space has been at war long enough that there are plenty of Earth ships of the *Jolly Jo's* age and general classification being salvaged and parted out."

An uncomfortable silence fell over everyone at the thought of making for a planet of unknown allegiance to obtain parts for the ship. But they knew as well as I did that we had no choice. I turned to the chief of security.

"Alex, I'm assigning security personnel to Dr. Brighton. Your staff will help collect and treat the rest of the wounded. Dr. Brighton, I know you're busy, but I'd like a list of our injured and lost. Get that to Commander Jacks as soon as possible. We need to get a handle on which of our crew members are available to us."

"Done, Captain." Menendez nodded.

The doctor winced and adjusted his freshly bandaged arm. "Thank You, Captain. I'll get that list compiled right away."

I nodded. "Since we have stabilized the ship and don't seem to have any Proximans pounding on our hatches at the moment, we need to take the opportunity to provide the crew with some much-needed rest. Gerdie, use the doctor's list and set up rotating port and starboard shifts to ensure coverage while allowing for solid rest periods. We don't need anyone making mistakes due to fatigue."

"Aye-aye, Captain." Her fingers were already flying over the face of her Comm Pad.

"Mr. Cathers, let's get this old girl moving before someone tries to sweep us up as junk. Maritime laws still apply in Earth space, but I've heard some nasty rumors about the laws of salvage being open to interpretation in this quadrant."

"Yes, sir."

* * *

Four hours later, we were lurching through space like a paraplegic turtle. I had been overly optimistic about our ability to maintain speed, but we were still on track to reach a nearby system before cataclysmic engine failure. I hoped.

We set course to the nearest planet, MX3314 in the star chart, Pilate to local navigators. The bridge had emptied, the crew settling into the new shift routine Gerdie had established. Gerdie was on a well-earned rest and ship's pilot Lieutenant Cathers was focused on maintaining course and monitoring engine speed, so he was no company at all. The lights were dimmed, and it was eerily quiet, making the bridge seem deserted.

I sat lost in my thoughts, the light bong of my communicator link in the captain's chair going unacknowledged, until I finally reached down and responded.

"Captain speaking. How may I help you today?" The was silence on the other end told me the caller wasn't sure they had reached the right place.

"Uh . . . Captain? This is Dr. Brighton, do you have a moment?"

"I do, Doctor. What can I do for you?"

"It would be best if we spoke in sick bay, I think."

"On my way." I glanced over at Cathers. "Mr. Cathers, can you manage?"

"Yes, Captain. I'll call if I need anything.

I made my way down to the sick bay. The crew had been working to clear debris as best they could, sweeping scattered scraps and components to the sides of the passageway. We didn't dare throw anything away. Aside from not wishing to leave any evidence of our current condition for our adversaries, we needed the raw materials. Even a singed control panel could be used to shore up a damaged bulkhead in a pinch.

As old as the *Jolly Jo* was, command looked the other way at some of the modifications we had made in our time aboard, such as the small smelting system and machine shops we had set up in an old storage bay. I took pride in knowing we were able to fabricate some repair parts ourselves, something our enemies could not do. The Proximans had a very different view. They were warriors, first and foremost, and while their weapons were of the highest caliber, their repair infrastructure was low priority. That was the one thing we had been able to take advantage of in this war, and likely one of the few things that had kept the human race from being overrun already.

To say that sick bay was full would be an understatement. Every available inch had been modified to accommodate crew members in various states of health, but the atmosphere was much calmer than on my earlier visit.

The doctor stood at the side of a crew member whose entire face was covered in bandages. He flicked his gaze on me as I entered and handed off his patient to one of the med techs.

"Captain, I sent the casualty list to Ms. Jacks as you asked," he said as he crossed the room, weaving around the wounded. "We've lost nearly 50 percent of the crew." He stared blankly, as if attempting to fathom the loss of life. We stood for a moment in silence.

"Doctor, I know this is your first chief medical officer assignment . . . " I said finally. I wasn't trying to be patronizing, I wanted to create some perspective for him.

His demeanor didn't change. "First deep space assignment, and my first combat," he said.

That was all I needed to know. It was a hell of a first day on the job. Even with all the years this crew and I had been fighting, this had been an especially nasty battle. I sympathized with the man, but I had no time to coddle him. "Doctor, was there something in particular you needed me for?"

He seemed to snap out of his malaise. "Yes, sir. I'm sorry, I'll try and stay focused. I wanted to review our medical status. I thought it best I not broadcast it over the intercom."

"Of course, a wise decision. No apologies necessary. This has been a tough one for all of us. You're doing fine."

Relief flickered across his face, then he frowned. "We're about out of everything. We've asked for blood donations from the remaining crew. We have crew members of all blood types, and the response has been good, but it's the physical supplies we need. Bandages, pain inhibitors, bone menders. I know you're looking for repair parts, but I wanted to ask—"

"Say no more." I interrupted. "I don't know what we'll be able to get, but if they take Earos, I keep plenty available to buy supplies with. And if they don't we'll just have to find something around here we can barter with. I have a few antiques in my quarters I'm sure somebody will find of value." I made a mental note to have Gerdie add time into the rotation to allow crew members to donate blood. Then I flashed the doctor a grin. "Compile a list of what you need and send it to me. I'll see what we can do once we arrive at the planet."

He tried his best to return the smile, but he was clearly exhausted. "Thank you, Captain. It's all on here." He handed me a pindrive and returned to treating his patients.

* * *

By the time we arrived within communications range of Pilate station, our scanners were nominally back online. The planet, as best we could tell, was managed from a large orbital station, which appeared to be a large, multilevel platform, much less haphazardly assembled than many of the other "neutral" planets we'd visited. Beyond the platform floated a vast army of ships in various states of disrepair, most likely salvage vessels towed here to be gutted for parts and sold off piecemeal.

There were a number of smaller ships shooting around the station, mostly transports with a few odd-looking vessels unlike any we had seen before. News of our battle must have arrived ahead of us and sent all the larger commerce ships in the area scrambling to get away from the danger, leaving the platform eerily alone where it hung above the planet.

The planet below looked inviting, everything a shade of blue. The planet was unable to support either human or Proximan life, which no doubt was to their benefit in this war. According to our meager database files, they did all their business with other races through the platform.

Lieutenant Markiers was working the patchwork communications board, sending a message to the platform that orbited the planet, hoping someone would reply. The planet was self-declared to be a unified world, but a lot of planets said that so they could get on the list of accepted trade destinations. As the front lines of the war had dragged back and forth across space, many of these colonies and planets found that both sides would honor a neutral declaration, and it was a good way to avoid becoming collateral damage.

The truth could have been something far different, from a fractioned, war-torn populace to a crime lord secret base, we had no idea what to expect. Unfortunately, we had no choice. We desperately needed repair parts and medical supplies.

"Attention Pilate Central Dock Control, this is the EDN *Johnathan Reilley* requesting permission to dock," Markiers repeated her request, and continued to receive to no answer.

Lieutenant Jooth waved me over to his navigation station. Gerdie followed. He spoke low. "Captain, when we lost long range sensors, I remembered the SSN that Earth deployed before sensor technology advanced far enough for ships to have their own networks . . . "

"SSN?" Gerdie gave me a puzzled look.

"Static Sensor Network. Old, seriously old school," I said. "Basically, Earth shot thousands of these sensor satellites through known space, to create a sort of grid that any ship could access if it were close enough to one of the satellites. Once crystal-based power had been refined and ships could carry their own equipment on board, they just let the grid go open source, and all sorts of races use it now."

Jooth interjected, "The satellites were built to be so durable, most of the ones that haven't been destroyed are still active."

"Your point, Mr. Jooth?" Gerdie said, impatience in her tone.

"I have been able to intermittently connect to the network. We don't have a lot of power, so I have to send the data in small bursts, and collect it as the network sends it back to me." He pointed to the screen in front of him. "I found the bad guys. They're coming after us."

I peered at the screen. The map of the sector blinked with the plotted path of an unidentified ship. Unknown to the SSN network maybe, but we knew damn well who it was.

"Based on what I see here, I am guessing we have maybe a couple of hours?" I was trying to make sense of the fragmented figures on the screen.

Gerdie saw the data and with her sharp mind did the calculation in short order. "At their current rate of speed, it's probably closer to three hours, which means they're probably just as banged up as we are."

"Let's not wait around and find out." I said just as the response from the planet came in.

"EDN *Johnathan Reilley,* you are cleared for shuttle embarkment. Please proceed to the coordinates provided on this secure data channel."

A palpable sense of relief washed over the bridge crew. I had no time to waste. "Gerdie, I need you to stay here."

"Sir—" she started to protest.

"Negative. We have a hostile three hours away, and we need a clear-headed leader on the bridge in case something happens."

She shot me a look of disgust, but said nothing.

"Nurstrang, how many operational shuttles do we have?"

"Three."

"Alright, Cathers, Menendez, and I will take one to the platform. Lieutenant Simmons, I need one in orbit that can handle the biggest possible payload, so as soon as we can strike a deal we can get everything loaded and back to the ship quick. Gerdie, keep track of my communicator signal. Move the *Jolly Jo* to a stationary orbital position on the opposite side of the planet from the approaching Proximan. Minimize transmissions. With any luck, they might think we moved on and just pass by." I got up to head to the transport car.

"Captain, you should let me go with you, I know what we need," Gerdie protested.

"I think I can handle a shopping list, Ms. Jacks. Besides, this might just be your chance to kick me to the curb."

She frowned at my poor attempt at humor.

"Cathers, Menendez, meet me in the shuttle bay in ten. I need to get my wallet." I stepped into the transport shaft. Gerdie followed.

"Going somewhere?" I asked, my hand hovering over the control panel.

"Maybe." She glared at me.

"Gerdie, look, if that Proximan ship gets here, only two people on this ship have the command ability to get the *Jolly Jo* out alive. I need you here." She knew I was right, but I knew she was as loyal and stubborn as they come. "I'm only going to say this once, and it is a direct order: If they show up, your priority is to get back to the rendezvous point. Understand?"

"Oh, I am not worried about leaving your ass here. I'll come back and kick it myself."

The door opened. "Take care of my ship," I told her.

"I'll take care of the ship, you just take care of yourself."

The door slid shut.

* * *

I hadn't had a chance to read the file on Pilate before we left in the shuttle, just scanned the headlines. It didn't really matter. Time was too short for true diplomacy. Anyway, with the war ravaging this sector for almost a year now, Pilate had to have been playing host to numerous traders and starships trying to stay out of the line of fire. Cathers piloted the shuttle, and Menendez sat in back, with me. The *Jolly Jo*, to her credit, had the old style shuttles designed for just this type of work. Built in a time when ships had to operate far from friendly facilities, the shuttles were bigger and better armed than newer models. I was glad I had bartered the last three shuttle upgrade orders into weapons upgrades, that was paying off handsomely. Menendez leaned back against the bulkhead, lost in his own thoughts.

"You alright?" I asked.

"I'm good, Captain. Tired, but good. But I am sure I don't have to tell you that." He smiled reassuringly.

"We'll be back before we know it—"

"Coming in, guys," Cathers interrupted.

With a shudder, the shuttle passed through the energy field that held in air and kept out space. The energy made my hair stand on end. I hated that. We glided to the pad, the shuttle gaining weight and dropping the last two feet with a thud.

"Cathers, we need to see about your pilot's license."

He started shutting down systems. "You're just soft riding in that big 'ole tin can all the time."

I stood up and activated the door panel. The door moved up, sliding inside the shuttle's bulkhead. With a whirring sound, the shuttle's steps deployed from beneath the hatch, and I stepped down. Cathers followed me out, stumbled, and fell forward.

"Hang on, there," I said, giving him a hand. "Gravity's stronger here than on the *Jo*."

"Thanks, Captain." He stood still for a moment, then took a couple of steps, getting used to the increased g-force.

The landing pad was a wide-open space, with a number of flared, steel-gray support beams spaced out across it. A few small ships and several shuttles sat on the pad, crews and attendants diligently working to refuel, repair, or otherwise handle their needs. No one paid us any attention. We were just another trader making a stop.

We waited.

After a few minutes, Menendez clomped down the stairs. "Where's the welcoming committee?" He shook his head and nearly lost his balance. "Man, less than a tenth G doesn't sound like much, but you really can feel the difference."

Cathers nodded. "Captain, I have the shuttle set to ping our communicators every twenty minutes, and relay tour locations to the *Jolly Jo*. They should be able to keep tabs on us pretty easily."

"All right. Let's move—"

Menendez touched my sleeve and motioned off to the right, where several dark figures stepped out from behind one of the support columns and headed in our direction. Out of instinct, my hand moved to the butt of my pistol and hovered there, at the ready.

Humanoid. Five of them. All armed. Four of them had gray skin and jet black hair. The fifth was cloaked and hooded. I could not make out any features. None of them had their weapons drawn, but my instinct told me to stay ready. They paused about five meters away from us. The cloaked figure reached slender gray hands to lift the hood, revealing the head of a woman, her gray skin several shades darker than the others, her hair twisted atop her head in ropy coils.

"I am Mehrdia, captain of the Pilate's guard. Please, identify your persons." She stared intently at us, obviously gauging our threat level.

I stepped forward. "My name is William Bordeaux, captain of the Earth Defense Network ship *Johnathan Reilley*. We seek the opportunity to trade or purchase parts to repair our vessel, as per the Neutral Systems Concord."

She quirked an eyebrow. Something I said had taken her by surprise, but I wasn't sure what.

"Captain Bordeaux, your reputation precedes you. To be clear, just as we must stand by the accord, we also have the right to refuse your request if it jeopardizes our station. We know that your ship is not alone."

I shifted uneasily. Time was wasting. She knew the Proximans were coming, and there was no leverage I could use to move the situation forward.

"With respect, Captain Mehrdia, we mean no harm to Pilate or its inhabitants. We need only a couple of Earth hours to secure and retrieve the supplies we need, and we can be on our way before our pursuers arrive."

"Captain Bordeaux, you shall have your two hours, but only that. Know that we have scanned your vessel and found it heavily damaged. If you are unable to leave orbit of this planet in those two Earth hours, we shall declare the ship salvage, claim it, and turn you and your crew over to the Proximans."

"I see. Is this the hospitality of Pilate?"

"It is for the protection of Pilate," she retorted. "If you have a better offer . . . " She allowed her words to trail off.

Point made. The look on Mehrdia's face told me my crew had kept their heads at her implied threat.

She turned to leave.

"Can you point me to the trade district?" I offered attempting to break the tension.

She waved her hand arbitrarily as she walked away, and disappeared behind a column, her guards following behind her.

* * *

The minutes ticked by as we divided the list between us, separating and trying to gather as much material as we could. My comm link buzzed with exchanges between the orbiting shuttle, Cathers, and Menendez as they made deals for equipment and swooped in and pick it up.

"Double scan everything for booby traps and bad software." It was all I could offer. I wasn't having much luck. I was working on the far more sensitive materials: medical supplies and rations. Whereas the guys could swap for parts with the local dealers, I had no such leverage. I was finding few medical installations at all, and fewer of them that wanted to sell what they had. I knew time was running out.

As I was leaving one more dealer empty handed, I found Mehrdia waiting for me.

"I believe I still have some time," I stated plainly, not in the mood to be pushed around.

"I am here to take you to the Station Magnate. He has requested your presence."

"With all due respect, I don't have time for diplomacy. Please apologize on my behalf."

She laughed. "You assume it's a choice. How quaint."

I realized she wasn't alone. Two station guards flanked her. Something was up. I reached up and flicked on my communicator. "Team, situation Brutus. I will be indisposed for a short time. Carry on."

A short cascade of "aye's" spat back through the comm as I joined Mehrdia. She made no threatening moves, but her backup fell smoothly in behind us as we walked.

"I assume this isn't a diplomatic visit," I said.

"It is not my job to make conversation, just to take you to the Magnate," she responded coolly, eyes straight ahead.

"I'm not sure if you don't like me, or if you're unhappy in your position," I responded with levity.

"How do you know it's not both?" We were silent the rest of the way.

A short time later, we entered a large room. A tall bank of monitors lined the opposite wall. I assumed they were monitoring the *Jolly Jo*. I wanted to confirm what they were gathering, but the monitors were too far away to tell. We had obviously entered the station's control room. A number of people milled about, working at various mundane tasks. To the right of the monitors, a huge window looked out over the curve of the planet and the space beyond.

"I'll take your weapon and communicator, please." Mehrdia stated sternly, extending her hand matter-of-factly.

I complied, handing her my Seron service phaser and communicator. Curiously, this was much more equipment and activity than a space station needed just to maintain a small trading post.

She scrutinized my weapon. "This isn't standard issue Earth defense weapon." she muttered.

"Neither am I." I retorted, my tone deadly serious.

Her head jerked up and I saw a flash of uncertainty in her eyes. She turned and placed my belongings on the table. A figure from across the room became aware of our presence, and turned.

"Ahh, Captain Bordeaux. Welcome to the Pilate station. Please join me."

I took my time crossing the room, trying to see what was on the monitors with my peripheral vision. He didn't look like a administrator. He wore a pale orange shirt, emblazoned with what I assumed was the station's logo, and work pants. His short hair was mussed, as if he hadn't bothered combing it.

"I'm sorry, should I know you?" I stopped a short distance from him and extended my hand. He looked at me with disgust and pulled his own hand tight to his side.

"My name is Maxstai, I am the Magnate of this station. It was I who summoned you."

"Thank you for the hospitality, Magnate Maxstai. What can I do for you?"

Close enough now to see some detail on the screens, I glanced at them. Most were status monitors for various parts of the station. I could only make out a few of the screens very clearly.

"You have sector scans of some pretty distant pieces of space from this station. Your command center here is damned impressive for a neutral station." I looked at the monitor with the blip of the Proximan cruiser on it. "I see you have a lock on our pursuer." There was no point in pretending not to notice, I assumed this must have fit into his agenda somehow.

He glanced at the vid screen, then smiled as he turned back to me. "Oh, we aren't worried about them. They won't be causing any harm. Tell me, how are your repairs proceeding? Was your ship terribly damaged in your battle in sector 24?" He raised an eyebrow.

I paused and looked around before answering. "I would imagine, Magnate Maxstai, based on this scanning equipment, that you already have the answer to your question."

I shifted, making note of who in the room had weapons. One of Maxstai's officers moved closer to him and whispered in his ear. His face to grew stern, almost angry, before he composed himself.

"Captain, let us dispense with the pleasantries, shall we? When you dropped your shields to give your shuttles access to your ship, we were able to get limited scans of your vessel. I almost know what I need to about how damaged it is. I'm not worried about Proximans. Let me offer you a way out of this situation that spares the remainder of your crew. If your ship were to, say, be listed as missing in action, and your remaining crew were to be saved by this station where the EDN could pick them up, there could be a benefit to you in addition to saving the lives of your crew."

I snuck a look at Mehrdia. She remained behind me, arms crossed, alert, but not particularly interested in what we were talking about. She seemed to be the only person armed. I turned my gaze back to Maxstai.

"How long have you been making offers like this, Mr. Maxstai?"

"Oddly enough, Captain Bordeaux, this is the first. Normally, no one is left alive for us to bargain with."

"You know salvaging Earth defense ships is considered an act of war?"

"Given that you cannot even handle the Proximans, I am not terribly worried about that." His tone was serious. He was done playing.

"I am going to have to respectfully decline, I'm afraid. I'm rather fond of my ship and my crew," I told him.

He considered his next move. "Most of you stupid navy types are."

Everything next happened all at once. Maxstai pulled a weapon and raised it. As he leveled it at me an alarm blared overhead. He hesitated just long enough for me to move out of the way. A beam shot past me within inches.

Mehrdia was caught off guard, and the beam grazed her shoulder. She hissed. The smell of burnt prylon fabric and singed flesh filled the room. She dived, rolled, and raised her weapon, but by the time she recovered, I had moved to disarm Maxstai. It was an easy task, since he had no military training. I smiled at Mehrdia, and pointed the magnate's own gun at his head.

"Now, Mehrdia, don't get too excited. I'm not looking to hurt anyone, I just want to get out of here."

"I hired you for security!" Maxstai spit out, disgusted.

"You know, Captain, I cannot let you do that." She rose to her feet slowly. "Your escape would be detrimental to my employment, not to mention my reputation."

Everyone else in the room froze, unsure of what to do. One of the men stationed in front of a live monitor started to call out, "Intru—"

The door at the far end of the room exploded in a hail of sparks and metal pieces. I pushed Maxstai to the floor, weapon still trained on him. Everyone else shielded their eyes. Mehrdia kept her weapon pointed at me, looking for an opportunity in the chaos to shoot or disarm me.

She never got the chance, and she soon found a Seron service phaser at the back of her head.

"I'll take that if you don't mind." Gerdie left no doubt she was serious.

Merhdia sighed, then offered up her weapon. Six of the *Jolly Jo's* security marines filtered in behind Gerdie, moving the occupants of the room together and scanning them for weapons. A marine took Maxstai off my hands and another took position behind Mehrdia, who had no interest in causing trouble. I stood up and moved to Gerdie.

"I told you I should have gone with." She half smiled. "I see you're making nice with the locals."

I chuckled. "It's my natural charm. Everybody okay?"

"Yes, sir. Cathers and Menendez got out as soon as you sent the signal. We didn't get much in the way of supplies, the station tried to sabotage us. We were lucky we caught the it at inspection. We also got a warning." Gerdie pulled a pad and tapped at it. I was perplexed.

"Who tipped you off? It wasn't me."

She looked me square in the eye. "It was the Proximans."

She moved toward the window before I could begin to process what she'd said. I just stood there, shaking my head.

"Time to go," Gerdie said. Mehrdia looked at her with indignation.

"Marines or not, you'll never make it back to the shuttle bay. I have well trained security, and you people are too moral to use us as shields." She let a little smug show. I looked over at Maxstai, and he was smiling at his improving situation. Gerdie pulled her phaser and adjusted its settings. She turned her back to the window and stared at Merhdia.

"Well, then, I guess we'll have to find another way." She let a little smug creep in herself.

Just then, behind Gerdie, the back side of a shuttle descended from above the window, filling it and blocking the light of the planet. It centered its rear door in the window after a moment, and extended a seal against the window with a dull thud.

Taking a step back, and turning to the window, Gerdie took aim with her service phaser.

She shot and cut a clean hole in it. Glass fell crashing to the floor.

Having been fully entertained, I turned my attention to a group huddled in the corner.

"Move these people into the hall, close the bulkhead after them." I pointed at Maxstai. "He goes with us."

I turned to Mehrdia. I could sense that she was expecting to be taken into custody as well.

"Mehrdia, I will be sending plenty of warships to take anyone left here into custody. I suggest a career change. You'll be much happier." She bowed her head slightly in understanding, then moved to the hall. I called after her.

"It was a pleasure meeting you."

"I cannot say the same, Captain." She didn't look back.

I ran to the table to collect my phaser and communicator. Gerdie had opened the shuttle door and a couple of marines had fashioned a crude set of steps from boxes and tables to allow easier access. Maxstai was whisked into the shuttle. The staff made their way into the hall, and we closed the bulkhead to the room, jamming the lock to buy some time.

The shuttle pulled away from the window, and there was a whoosh of air and debris getting sucked out of the room through the hole we left behind. We made our way back to the *Jolly Jo.*

"Your friend here," Gerdie offered, jutting her chin at Maxstai, "has apparently been salvaging and murdering indiscriminately for some time. There is a boneyard of ships on the far side of the planet. Earth, Proximan, you name it. Some are ships we've been looking for for a while."

I looked at Maxstai. He leaned in. "It's war. And I'm a businessman."

* * *

Once back on the *Jolly Jo*, things were hopping by the time we got to the bridge. I settled awkwardly in the leaning captain's chair. "What's the situation, Lieutenant Nurstrang?"

"Two large ships have emerged from the back side of the planet. Heavily armed. Both the same size as the *Jolly Jo*. On course to pursue."

"Lieutenant Jooth, change course to the rendezvous point, best possible speed."

"Aye," Jooth confirmed.

"Nurstrang, what do we have for weapons?"

"Missles at command, three of nine tubes available. You have seven shots. Captain, I have analyzed their weapons, and they could definitely outgun us, even if we were at full capacity. We still have no energy weapons."

I turned to Gerdie. "Maxstai said something about wanting to see if we were damaged enough."

She leaned toward me a hint, but remained fixed on the view screen. "I'm guessing because they didn't want us to shoot back?"

"That doesn't make sense, those ships outgun us even at full capacity. He was looking for something specific." I closed my eyes in thought.

Jooth broke my concentration. "Captain, two minutes until the ships are in range to fire on us."

Gerdie moved over to the weapons console with Nurstrang. "We have 15 percent shield strength, that should—"

"Wait," I interrupted Gerdie, standing up and moving over to the station, "do they have shields?"

Nurstrang tapped into the sensor array. "If they do, they haven't put them up." The lights went on in their eyes even before I made it back to the chair to call engineering.

"Engineering. This is the captain."

"Lieutenant Simmons, Captain. Your engines are giving as much as they can, sir."

"I know Lieutenant. I need to know how fast you van get an EMP mine deployed."

"Ah . . . what . . . ? When you give the word."

"Weapons control is going to synchronize its release with a weapons launch. Await their command."

"Aye," came the signal.

I turned to Gerdie. She didn't even wait for me to say anything. She turned to Nurstrang.

"Cue two missiles, synchronize their launch and the release of the EMP mine."

I turned to Markiers. "I need electronic counter measures activated now. I also want tons of electronic noise, make it seem like all our equipment is overloading. We have to confuse their sensors as much as possible."

She turned to her console. "Aye, Captain, but we won't be able to see or hear much ourselves while I do it."

"That's okay." I turned to Nurstrang while Gerdie made her way back to the command chair.

"Launch on my command, Luieutenant."

"Understood. Ready, Captain."

"One Minute to weapons range, Captain," said Cathers.

The screen started to experience the interference from the electric noise we were making. The silhouettes of the ships were soon lost in flashing screen snow.

"Now, Nurstrang. How are shields?"

"Holding at 15 percent."

We could feel the missiles slightly as they launched from their tubes. Gerdie looked down at the floor. "I never would have thought of this."

"You will one day, when you're a captain."

The seconds dragged by in an eternity. After about 45 seconds, we felt the slight push of the EMP pulse wash over the ship. Everything flickered for just a moment.

"Hold on, old girl. . . . Hold on." I whispered to the air.

Everything held.

I sat in the chair. "Markiers, cut the clatter. Jooth, get me an assessment of what's going on out there."

As the electric noise faded, the view screen came back online, showing a background of stars. Everyone was silent, peering intently at the screen for any sign of our pursuers.

"Did we get them, Jooth?" I whispered as I searched. Jooth took his time responding, double checking his readings.

"We got 'em. They are out there, dead in space. Dead enough anyway." The relief was audible, with several crew members quietly vocalizing their happiness. Jooth followed up, "They took out the missiles like you expected. It looks like we created enough electronic noise they never saw the EMP mine, or they assumed it was a piece of the ship."

I looked around, stood up. "Markiers, call senior staff to a briefing in Conference Room Two. Maintain red alert, the Pilates may have another trick up their sleeves."

Minutes later, with everyone assembled in the conference room, we reviewed our status. We still had a Proximan cruiser bearing down on us, and we were in no condition to fight it off.

"Once you left for the station, Captain, we got a communication," Markiers offered. "Very narrow band, someone trying not to draw attention to themselves. Text only. 'Pilate a trap. Do not stop.' That was when I traced it to the Proximan ship."

"I was able to determine that the Proximan ship wasn't under its own power," Jooth pitched in the next piece of the puzzle. "It was being towed. There are three Shotah class transports towing it. They're taking it back to the station, probably to disassemble it."

"What about the Proximans?" I asked.

She looked puzzled, "I can only assume that the Pilates tracked the Proximan ship after our battle, boarded the vessel, and have done their best to kill off the remaining Proximans."

I thought about this. "Do we have a way of getting a message back to them?"

"I have all the details of their communication to us," Markiers said. "We could send a message back. But unless they respond, we'd never know if they got it. And, of course, the Pilate vessels will get it as well."

"We'll have to take that chance," I said.

Gerdie's jaw dropped.

"So, let me get this right, we just spent three days, getting the crap kicked out of us by

Proximans—these Proximans—and we lost over half our crew. Now you want to save them from a bunch of space pirates? Really?!" She stared, doing everything she could to control her frustration.

Everyone else shifted uneasily. It was clear they weren't sure how they felt about it. Gerdie had no doubts. Neither did I.

"Markiers, set up a communications connection using a Proximan code, use one that the Proximans know we have broken, but that the Pilate most likely won't know. Simmons, get me a systems update as soon as possible, I need to know what we have. Jooth, keep us on a course back to rendezvous with the *Richard* and the *Misery*. That will take us in weapons range of the oncoming ships. Sitting here just makes us a target for the station and those two cruisers when they get up and running." Everyone acknowledged and made their way out.

"Commander Jacks, a word." She stayed in the room, looking at the door as the last of the staff left.

She sighed heavily. "I'm s—"

"Stow the sorries, Gerdie, I know you better than that."

She spun around, pointing at the bulkhead. "This is a war, in case you haven't figured it out yet. These are the bad guys. Call me crazy, but winning a war usually means killing more bad guys than they kill of your guys. We should let them die! The Pilates are doing us a favor."

I sighed, folding my hands on the table while I formulated a response. "You know what, if the situation were reversed, and it was us fighting off a boarding party, and we called to a nearby Proximan

108

ship, they would come running just so they could
blow us up out of principle."

A puzzled look flashed across Gerdie's face.

"My point is this. Change doesn't happen
until someone makes it happen. You and I both
know that the Proximans do not ask for help, even
from each other. The last thing they do is talk to
their enemies at all. Ever. They are ruthless,
destructive, and clinically military.

"If this is legit, and they do want our help,
and we extend that help . . . Think about it. This
whole war changes."

Gerdie sat down and looked at me.

"You are dreaming."

I leaned in.

"You can have me removed from command. I
think Brighton would sign off."

She laughed and leaned back. I pressed the
point.

"If we don't try this, if we don't try, when will
this end? How many more of our friends are we
going to have to say goodbye to?"

She glanced away, pondering, then turned
and leaned in toward me. "Bill, I have never had
someone in my life that I've trusted more than you.
I would never try to have you removed from
command. But these people are exhausted. We
have pushed them too far for too long. We need to
get them home. We need to end this. We're not
diplomats. We're not going to end this war here,
even if we save a few bloodthirsty Proximans." She
sagged, lowering her head to the table. I reached
out and put a hand on her shoulder. She raised her
head. Her eyes met mine.

"Gerdie, don't you get it? This war isn't going to end until enough of us on both sides realize how fruitless it is. If we have the opportunity to change just one mind, just one Proximan's perception of us—isn't that worth the risk to save billions? Don't you think everyone on this ship gets that?"

She sighed. She raised the corner of her mouth. "I hate you so much right now."

"You should have let them kill me in the station."

"I can't stand the thought of having to train a new captain." She stood up and headed for the door, pausing. "I'm kind of fond of the one I already have."

* * *

The news from Lieutenant Evans in damage control was better than expected. We had restored 50 percent ion power, stabilized the life support, and reconnected some semblance of weapons control. As I sat on the bridge, Lieutenant Markiers worked to connect us with the Proximans, while Gerdie and Lieutenant Jooth attempted to use the SSN Network to learn more about the Pilates and their Proximan captives.

"Captain, I have the Proximans. Audio only," Markiers finally proclaimed.

"Lieutenant, is the translator working? Can you feed it through?"

"Yes, sir, feeding now."

Everyone stopped. The speakers crackled before going quiet. After the silence, there came a sequence of guttural tones and noises, followed by the computer's voice translation.

"Attention Earth ship. This is Squadron Captain Irgh of the Proximan vessel *Groma*."

"Proximan vessel, this is the Earth ship *Johnathan Reilley*, commanded by Captain William Bordeaux," I responded. "Please state your status, Captain Irgh."

There was a long silence. It could have been due to translation delay, or they were trying to formulate an answer. I didn't wait.

"Captain Irgh, please accept my gratitude for the information regarding our mutual problem. Can we assist your vessel at this time?"

There was another long silence. Everyone could feel the tension in the room and looked at each other nervously. Only hours before, Proximans were the enemy. These aliens had tried to kill us.

Then came the droning answer. "Earth ship *Johnathan Reilley*, we respectfully request that you destroy the *Groma*, with all hands aboard."

Gerdie's forehead wrinkled almost approvingly.

"Proximan honor code. They don't want to ask for our help. They would rather die," I said, to no one in particular.

"Earth ship *Johnathan Reilley*, we request that you destroy this vessel," the communication continued."We are unable to retake command. The scavengers have invaded our vessel and driven us to the lower decks. Our ship and crew must not be plundered. It dishonors us and our lineage. Please comply."

"Proximan vessel, we believe we can defeat the scavengers and return control of your ship to you. We can assist with the medical needs of your crew until your rescue ships arrive."

"Earth ship *Johnathan Reilley*, we refuse your assistance. We have no rescue options. We are sending you the coordinates for the reactor core of this vessel to target. Please comply."

I dug desperately for some way to reach him. I stood up, staring intently at the view screen, my voice growing louder and more frantic. "Captain Irgh, we do not have to be enemies. We can help each other. You chose to help us, let us choose to help you now."

"Our choice was of necessity. A need greater than our enmity. A need we ask you to now fulfill."

"Captain," interrupted Jooth, "two of the Pilate ships are breaking off and heading this way. They're on to us."

"Armament, Mr., Jooth?"

"They're damned well-armed. Proximan laser mounts and two atomic missile launchers per ship. They've been scavenging the weapons systems of ships on both sides, and they've made some major modifications."

"Nurstrang, load missiles. Target the coordinates provided by the Proximans. Prepare to launch."

"Aye, Captain."

The red alert klaxon sounded. The crew, having been standing and listening to the interaction, snapped to the moment and scurried across the bridge.

The Proximans responded.

"Earth ship *Johnathan Reilley*, we have no rescue options. Understand that this is the choice we make. Entreat your compliance."

"Nurstrang, do you have them?"

"In range and locked on, Captain."

Gerdie's eyes remained fixed on the view screen, unwavering. As much as she trusted me, she wanted to see this last Proximan ship destroyed, the mission completed, the victory complete.

I set my jaw. "Fire."

"Missiles away, Captain. Twenty seconds— fifteen Proximan cycles—to impact." I motioned to Markiers to reconnect the Proximans.

"This is the Earth ship *Johnathan Reilley*. We have complied. Missiles will impact in 12 of your cycles. There is still time for us to terminate and rescue—"

"Earth ship *Johnathan Reilley*, thank you for your compliance. You have our gratitude. We are allies this day." Then silence of a dead circuit.

It was forever, and no one on the bridge dared make eye contact with anyone else as it played out.

"Missile impact," Nurstrang reported.

The *Jo* shifted. I took a step to steady myself, the shock wave nudging the old warship as it rolled over her. Once the ship settled, the bridge crew was silent except for the klaxon of the alert that still screeched from all sides.

"Captain, the Pilate ships are slowing. It would appear they were damaged in the Proximans' blast. The Proximans appear to have padded the explosion with other explosives of their own. Looks like the Pilates are heading back to the station."

"Mr. Jooth, keep us moving to the rendezvous point. Nurstrang, load two more missiles in case the Pilates get any bright ideas.

And someone turn off that damned alarm. I'll be somewhere . . . quiet." No one spoke as I left the bridge.

* * *

Hours later, I had found a quiet space in the keel, the very bottom of the ship. There was no window, no expanse of space to stare into. Just the dull metal of the hull and the hum of the ship, quiet and low. She was hurting, but she still sounded and felt vibrant, alive. Despite everything we had put her through, she had never given up. She always gave us just enough to escape death, again and again. People had called her the miracle worker long before I had taken command.

Jolly Jo had been named originally for twentieth century admiral, Johnathan Reilley. He was a nobody, an ensign stationed on Neptune. He worked alone in a remote-controlled defense satellite and drone network that had been deemed redundant and was scheduled to be shut down.

When the Proximans disabled the main outer solar system defense network on their way to Earth, Reilley held off the entire fleet with a bunch of old satellites and drones. Because of him, Earth was saved. The first failed invasion in the history of the Proximan Empire.

"Is this seat taken?" Gerdie spoke cautiously, but she slid down to sit beside me before I could respond.

"We've increased power by another ten percent, all engines are now engaged, and the *Richard* will be coming alongside to escort us back to Starbase 22. *Misery* is going to go straight to Pilate, to rendezvous with a Proximan ship."

"Not funny," I told her.

"Oh, that's right, there are no comm stations down here, so you haven't see this." She handed me a communications pad.

"The Proximans sent this out right before they were destroyed. It was a different encryption code, one I don't think they knew we had cracked. Apparently this Irgh guy wasn't just captain of the *Groma*, he was the commander of the whole squadron we defeated."

I read the pad.

"Most exalted commanders,

Know per orders delivered 8642.234 our squadron engaged the Earthers' main battleship in the sector HGMR. The squadron fought valiantly, but all ships were lost except Groma. Following the battle, the Pilate scourge attempted to commandeer Groma and murder its crew.

Honorably, the exalted Earther ship allied with us to defeat the pirates' plans. It is my opinion that the Eathers may be approachable as a non-lesser species.

I passed in honor to The Higher Place.

Commander Irgh"

I stared at it. Gerdie talked on.

"Anyway, about an hour later, the *Jolly Jo* called us, and said the Proximans had contacted command to ask about cooperating and going after the pirates. Apparently, your little buddy we captured has been working overtime. He's slaughtered the crews of wounded Proximan ships with those two home-made battle cruisers and dragged their hulls back to Pilates, scavenging them and selling the parts to the highest bidder. They sent us a whole bunch of intel they have collected on these guys. They think your girlfriend is the ring leader. I knew I should have shot her."

I handed the comm pad back to her. Gerdie sat next to me for a minute, as if she was trying to see what I saw in the bulkhead wall, even tilting her head at one point. Finally, she gave up and got to her feet.

"So, you can either get your ass up, and be the freaking captain of this 'most exalted Earther main battleship,' and give me shit because you were right, or you can be a mopey little boy down here for whatever reason I have no clue."

She extended her hand. I took it and stood.

"Thank you for the trust."

"Oh, don't get me wrong. I think you're a nut case. But you're my Captain Nutcase."

I smiled as we headed up the ladder and back to the transport shaft that would take us to the bridge.

More Brick Cave Books by
Sharon Skinner

The Healer's Legacy
ISBN: 9781938190025

The Matriarch's Devise
ISBN: 9781938190285

Mirabella and the Faded Phantom
ISBN: 9781938190162

The Nelig Stones
ISBN: 9781938190131

FORTHCOMING:
Collars & Curses
Supernal Dawn (with J.A. Giunta)
The Chronicles of Tavara Tinker:
The Black Airship (With Bob Nelson)

More Brick Cave Books by
J.A. Giunta

The Last Incarnation
ISBN: 9781938190230

The Mists of Faeron
ISBN: 9781938190070

Out of the Dark
ISBN: 9781938190155

Knights of Virtue
ISBN: 9781938190049

FORTHCOMING:
Supernal Dawn (with Sharon Skinner)

The Warden's Legacy
More Brick Cave Books by
Scott Woods

We Over Here Now
ISBN: 9781938190117

Urban Contemporary History Month
ISBN: 9781938190308

FORTHCOMING:
Cthuhlu Dayz

More Brick Cave Books by
Colette Black

FORTHCOMING:
Moon Shadows

More Books by
Bob Nelson

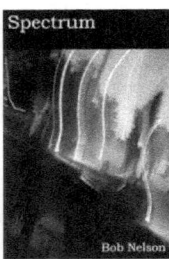

Spectrum
ISBN: N/A Amazon only

The Chronicles of Tavara Tinker
Le Tour de Paris
ISBN: 9781938190148
(With Sharon Skinner)

The Chronicles of Tavara Tinker:
The Sounds of Time
ISBN: 9781938190193
(With Sharon Skinner)

The Stories of Haven: I
ISBN:
(With Sharon Skinner, J.A. Giunta, Nick Ozment)

FORTHCOMING:
The Chronicles of Tavara Tinker:
The Black Airship (With Sharon Skinner)
Sacrifice
Subterfuge

About Brick Cave

The mission of BCM is to effectively support the creative endeavors of talented individuals that they may realize a benefit beyond the creative process. Our aim is to leverage technology, and the changes in media availability of the last ten years to make a market for the endeavors of our artists.

Founded in 2006. BCM has created a full-length feature film (Sacrifice, 2010), produced several spoken word albums and published over 40 books to date.

The organization continues to seek new ways to create and publish media and can be found online at brickcavemedia.com.